George Frederick Pardon

Backgammon and Draughts (or checkers)

George Frederick Pardon

Backgammon and Draughts (or checkers)

ISBN/EAN: 9783337600099

Printed in Europe, USA, Canada, Australia, Japan

Cover: Foto ©Andreas Hilbeck / pixelio.de

More available books at **www.hansebooks.com**

BACKGAMMON

AND

DRAUGHTS

(*OR CHECKERS*)

COMPRISING G. F. PARDON'S COMPLETE WORK.
AND MANY VALUABLE PARTS OF ANDREW
ANDERSON'S "CHECKERS."

NEW YORK
FREDERICK A. STOKES COMPANY
PUBLISHERS

CONTENTS.

—

BACKGAMMON.

—

DRAUGHTS.

PREFACE.

BACKGAMMON remains in precisely the condition in which it was left over a hundred years ago, by "Edmond Hoyle, Gent." In this short account of the game are given the preliminary instructions which Hoyle and others almost invariably omit. Hoyle presumes on his reader's general knowledge of the manner of playing the various games, and begins his account of Backgammon with a calculation of chances and a table of odds against throwing certain numbers on two dice. This, the mere gambling element of the game, is not primarily necessary for the amateur's instruction. When he knows how to play Backgammon, he will soon acquire facility in making wagers on his success. It is a pleasant evidence of advancement in morals, that most of the games our forefathers played for heavy stakes are now ordinarily played "for love." Chess, Draughts, Backgammon, Whist, and most of the card games, are better played for amusement than for money.

BACKGAMMON.

BACKGAMMON and Draughts go very well together, for almost all the folding Draught-boards contain a Backgammon-board inside.

As to the origin of the game there is little to be said, except that it was known to our Saxon ancestors, as a game of mingled chance and skill. Strutt and Bishop Kennett derive its name from two Saxon words—*bac*, back; and *gamen*, a game—a back-game, or one in which the player is liable to be sent back. Dr. Henry and other writers claim for it a purely Welsh origin, and say that its name comes from *back*, little; and *cammon*, a battle—the little battle. Chaucer called it Tables, by which title the game seems to have been known in his time. As to the Draught-men and dice with which it is played, of the introduction of the first we have no certain knowledge; and with regard to the spotted cubes, their origin cannot now be traced to any one people. Representations of dice are seen in Egyptian hieroglyphs and on Etruscan tombs. It has always been a game for the higher classes, and has never been vulgarized or defiled by uneducated people. Bacon, the philosopher, recommends it as a good game; Shakspeare draws morals from its chances; Spenser mentions dice in his "Faërie Queene"; Addison, Dryden, and other writers mention it as a gentlemanly pastime; and Dean Swift tells us that it is the only game that a clergyman can consistently play!

Backgammon is played by two persons on a board divided into two sections, and figured with twenty-four points or flèches, of different colors, placed alternately. Here is the board, with the men arranged for the game:

BLACK.

Black's Home, or Inner Table.   Black's Outer Table.

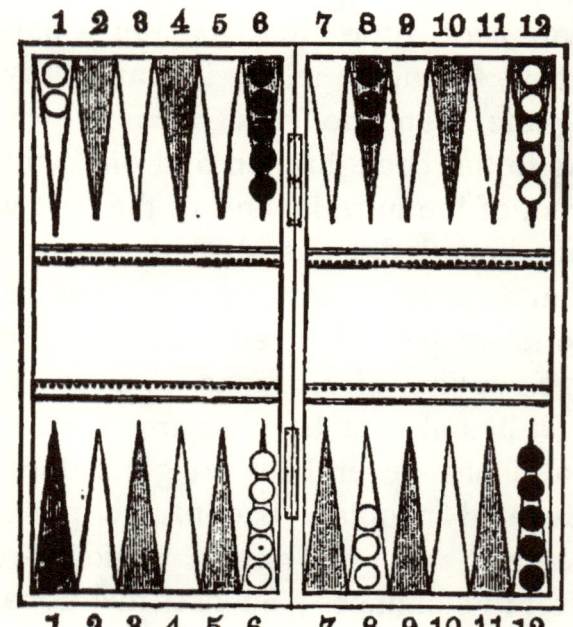

White's Home, or Inner Table.   White's Outer Table.

WHITE.

The very first thing is to "set the board," which is done according to the scheme shown in the diagram, in which for easy reference the points on either side are numbered from 1 to 12. The player using the black men is seated at the upper side of the table, and the one with the white men at the lower. In the case supposed, it is the object of the player to bring all his men "home"; that is, into his own inner table. He who first succeeds in moving or "bearing" his men off the board, wins the game. In arranging the board, two men are placed upon the ace-point in the adversary's inner table, five upon the sixth point of his outer table (12 in the diagram), five upon the sixth point in your own inner table, and three upon the cinque point in your outer table (8 in the diagram). Your adversary places his men in the tables in a precisely corresponding manner.

The moves of the men are made in accordance with the numbers thrown by two dice, with which, in a box, each player is provided, in addition to fifteen draughtmen.

To further explain the *motif* of the game. It is the object of the player to get all his men into his inner compartment or "home," and "bear" or remove them from the board in accordance with the numbers indicated by the successive throws of the dice, before his adversary can accomplish the same end, after he has succeeded in removing his men into his own " home." But before going farther, it will be well to explain the

TECHNICAL TERMS OF THE GAME.

The terms used for the numbers on the dice are— 1, *ace ;* 2, *deuce;* 3, *trois*, or *tray ;* 4, *quatre ;* 5, *cinque ;* 6, *six.*

Doublets.—Two dice with the faces bearing the same number of pips, as two aces, two sixes, etc.

Bearing your Men.—Removing them from the table.

Hit.—To remove all your men before your adversary has done so.

Blot.—A single man upon a point.

Home.—Your inner table.

Gammon.—Two points won out of the three constituting the game.

Backgammon.—The entire game won.

Men.—The draughts used in the game.

Making Points.—Winning hits.

Getting Home.—Bringing your men from your opponent's tables into your own.

To Enter.—Is to place your man again on the board after he has been excluded by reason of a point being already full.

Bar.—The division between the boxes.

Bar-point.—That next the bar.

Having got thus far, let us see

HOW THE GAME IS PLAYED.

The first most advantageous throw of the dice is of aces, as it blocks the six-point in your outer table, and secures the cinque-point in your inner table; so that your adversary's two men upon your ace-point cannot escape with his throwing either from five or six. This throw is, therefore, often asked and given between players of unequal skill, by way of odds.

If doublets are thrown, or similar numbers on each die, double the number of points are reckoned. Thus, if two cinques be thrown, twenty points are counted.

The points on the board are counted from one to six in each of the four compartments respectively, each player commencing from the point in the table opposite to him.

Two men can be advanced at once, one for each number thrown on the dice; or one man may be moved forward as many points as the numbers on the dice amount to, taken together.

When any point is covered by two of an opponent's men, the player cannot put any of his upon that point; but if one only be there, which constitutes what is called "a blot," that man may be removed and placed on the centre ledge of the board, and the point occupied. This man must be "entered" on any vacant point in the "home" section of the tables belonging to the opponent of the player whose man has been taken up, provided the number turned up on either die corresponds with that point, and must then be brought round from the commencement, like the men on the ace-points in either table.

To win a "hit" is to remove all your men from the table before your adversary has removed his : this counts one. To win a "gammon," which counts two, is to remove all your men before your adversary has brought all of his "home"; and if your men are entirely removed while your antago-nist has one remaining in your home section of the tables, you win a "backgammon," which counts three.

For the choice of the first play, each player throws a single die. "He who throws the highest number wins, and may, if he choose, adopt and play the joint number of the preliminary throw. If he reject, then the first step is made by his throw-ing both the dice, and moving any one of his men to an open point at the distance indicated by one of the dice. and then moving another man (or the same man farther on, if he think proper) to another open point indicated by the number of the second die.

This completes his move; his adversary then follows in a similar manner, and so on alternately to the end of the game. Thus, double aces (which count as 4) would entitle you (say White) to move two men from 8 w. to 7 w., and two from 6 w. to 5 w., which covers the bar-point (7), and also covers the cinque point in your inner table, and then, should your next throw be 5 and 6, you would play the five from 12 b. to 8 w., and so cover the blot before left; and you would play the six from 12 b. to your bar-point. Pairs count double; thus, sixes entitle you to move four men, each six points forward, and you may either move four together, say, from 12 b. to 7 w., or two together, as, say, two from 1 b. to your adversary's bar-point (7), and two from 12 b. to 7 w. (your own bar-point), or singly—as, say, a single man from 1 b. to 1 w. in your own inner table, presuming that your adversary had ceased to occupy it."

The direction in which your men move is from the adverse inner table over the bar, through the adversary's outer table.

HOYLE'S HINTS, OBSERVATIONS, AND CAUTIONS.

By the directions given to play for a gammon, you are voluntarily to make some blots; the odds being in your favor that they are not hit; but should that so happen, in such case you will have three

men in your adversary's table; you must then endeavor to secure your adversary's cinque, quatre,
or trois-point, to prevent a gammon, and must be
very cautious how you suffer him to take up a fourth
man.

Take care not to crowd your game, that is, putting many men either upon your trois or deuce-
point in your own table ; which is, in effect, losing
those men by not having them to play.   Besides,
by crowding your game, you are often gammoned ;
as, when your adversary finds your game open by
being crowded in your own table he may then
play as he thinks fit.

By referring to the calculations, you may know
the odds of entering a single man upon any certain
number of points, and play your game accordingly.

If you are obliged to leave a blot, by having
recourse to the calculations for hitting it, you will
find the chances for and against you.

You will also find the odds for and against being
hit by double dice, and consequently can choose a
method of play most to your advantage.

If it be necessary to make a run, in order to win
a hit, and you would know who is forwardest, begin
reckoning how many points you have to bring home
to the six-point in your table the man that is at the
greatest distance, and do the like by every other
man abroad ; when the numbers are summed up,

add for those already on your own tables (supposing the men that were abroad as on your six-point for bearing), namely, six for every man on the six, and so on respectively for each ; five, four, three, two, or one, for every man according to the points on which they are situated. Do the like to your adversary's game, and then you will know which of you is forwardest, and likeliest to win the hit.

DIRECTIONS FOR BEARING YOUR MEN.

If your adversary be greatly before you, never play a man from your quatre, trois or deuce points, in order to bear that man from the point where you put it, because nothing but high doublets can give you any chance for the hit ; therefore, instead of playing an ace or a deuce from any of the aforesaid points, always play them from your highest point ; by which means, throwing two fives, or two fours, will, upon having eased your six and cinque points, be of great advantage : whereas, had your six point remained loaded, you must perhaps be obliged to play at length those fives and fours.

Whenever you have taken up two of your adversary's men, and happen to have two, three or more points made in your own table, never fail spreading your men, either to take a new point in your table, or to hit the man your adversary may happen to enter. As soon as he enters one, compare his game with yours; and if you find your game equal, or better, take the man if you can, because it is twenty-five to eleven against his hitting you; which being so much in your favor, you ought always to run that risk, when you have already two of his men up : except you play for a single hit only.

Never be deterred from taking up any one man of your adversary by the apprehension of being hit with double dice, because the fairest probability is five to one against him.

If you should happen to have five points in your table, and to have taken up one of your adversary's men, and are obliged to leave a blot out of your table, rather leave it upon doublets than any other, because doublets are thirty-five to one against his hitting you, and any other chance is but seventeen to one against him.

Two of your adversary's men in your table are better for a hit than any greater number, provided your game be the forwardest; because having three or more men in your table gives him more chances to hit you, than if he had only two men.

If you are to leave a blot upon entering a man on your adversary's table, and have your choice where, always choose that point which is the most disadvantageous to him. To illustrate this : suppose it is his interest to hit or take you up as soon as you enter ; in that case leave the blot upon his lowest point; that is to say, upon his deuce, rather than upon his trois, and so on ; because all the men your adversary plays upon his trois or his deuce points are in a great measure out of play, these men not having it in their power to make his cinque-point, and consequently his game will be crowded there and open elsewhere, whereby you will be able also much to annoy him.

Prevent your adversary from bearing his men to the greatest advantage, when you are running to save a gammon : suppose you should have two men upon his ace-point, and several others abroad ; though you should lose one point or two, in putting the men into your table, yet it is your interest to leave a man upon the adversary's ace-point, which will prevent him bearing his men to his greatest advantage, and will also give you the chance of his making a blot, that you may hit. But if, upon calculation, you find you have a throw, or a probability of saving your gammon, never wait for a blot, because the odds are greatly against hitting it.

THE LAWS OF BACKGAMMON.

If you take a man or men from any point, that man or men must be played.

You are not understood to have played any man till it is placed upon a point, and quitted.

If you play with fourteen men only, there is no penalty attending it, because with a lesser number you play to a disadvantage, by not having the additional man to make up your tables.

If you bear any number of men before you have entered a man taken up, and which, consequently, you were obliged to enter, such men, so borne, must be entered again in your adversary's tables, as well as the man taken up.

If you have mistaken your throw, and played it, and your adversary have thrown, it is not in your power or his choice to alter it, unless both parties agree.

The following are Hoyle's

GENERAL INSTRUCTIONS.

If you play three up at Backgammon, your principal view, in the first place, is to secure your own, or your adversary's cinque-point, or both; when that is effected, you may play a pushing game, and endeavor to gammon your adversary.

The next best point (after you have gained your cinque-point) is to make your bar-point, thereby preventing your adversary's running out with doublet sixes.

When you have proceeded thus far, prefer the

making your quatre-point in your own tables, rather than the quatre-point out of them.

Having gained these points, you have a fair chance to gammon your adversary, if he is very forward : for, suppose his tables are broke at home, it will be then your interest to open your bar-point, and to oblige him to come out of your tables with a six ; and having your men spread, you not only may catch that man which your adversary brings out of your tables, but you will also have a probability of taking up the man left in your tables (upon supposition that he has two men there.) If he should have a blot at home, it will then be your interest not to make up your tables ; because, if he should enter upon a blot, which you are to make for the purpose, you will have a probability of getting a third man ; which, if accomplished, will give you at least 4 to 1 of the gammon ; whereas, if you have only two of his men up, the chances are that you do not gammon him.

If you play for a hit only, one or two men taken up by your adversary renders it surer than a greater number, provided your tables are made up.

Hoyle gives the following directions for

PLAYING AT SETTING OUT THE THIRTY-SIX CHANCES OF THE DICE FOR A GAMMON OR A SINGLE HIT.

Two aces—best of first throws to be played on

your cinque-point ; and then two on the bar-point for a gammon, or for a hit.

Two sixes (second best throw) to be played ; two on your adversary's bar-point, and two on your bar-point, for a gammon or a hit.

Two trois, two to be played on the cinque-point, and the other two on your trois-point in your own tables, for a gammon only.

Two deuces, to be played on the quatre-point in your own tables, and two are brought over from the five men placed in your adversary's outer tables, for a gammon only.

Two fours, to be brought over from the five men placed in your adversary's outer tables, and to be put upon the cinque-point in your own tables, for a gammon only.

Two fives, to be brought over from the five men placed in your adversary's outer tables, and to be put on the trois-point in your own tables, for a gammon or a hit.

Size ace, you are to make your bar-point, for a gammon or for a hit.

Size deuce, a man to be brought from the five men placed in your adversary's outer tables, and to be placed on the cinque-point in your own tables, for a gammon or a hit.

Six and three, a man to be brought from your adversary's ace-point, as far as he will go, for a gammon or a hit.

Six and four, a man to be brought from your adversary's ace-point, as far as he will go, for a gammon or a hit.

Six and five, a man to be carried from your adversary's ace-point, as far as he can go, for a gammon or a hit.

Cinque and quatre, a man to be carried from your adversary's ace-point, as far as he can go, for a gammon or a hit.

Cinque-trois, to make the trois-point in your table, for a gammon or a hit.

Cinque-deuce, to play two men from the five placed in your adversary's outer tables, for a gammon or a hit.

Cinque-ace, to bring one man from the five placed in your adversary's outer tables for the cinque, and to play one man down on the cinque-point in your own tables for the ace, for a gammon only.

Quatre-trois, two men to be brought from the five placed in your adversary's outer tables, for a gammon or a hit.

Quatre-deuce, to make the quatre-point in your own tables, for a gammon or a hit.

Quatre-ace, to play a man from the five placed in your adversary's outer tables for the quatre, and for the ace, to play a man down upon the cinque-point in your own tables, for a gammon only.

Trois-deuce, two men to be brought from the five placed in your adversary's tables, for a gammon only.

Trois-ace, to make the cinque-point in your own tables, for a gammon or a hit.

Deuce-ace, to play one man from the five placed in your adversary's tables for the deuce ; and for the ace, to play a man down upon the cinque-point in your own tables, for a gammon only.

HOW TO PLAY FOR THE FOLLOWING CHANCES WHEN YOU PLAY ONLY FOR A HIT.

Two trois, two of them are to be played on your cinque-point in your own tables, and with the other two take the quatre-point in your adversary's tables.

Two deuces, two of them are to be played on your quatre-point in your own tables, and with the other two take the trois-point in your adversary's tables.

[The two foregoing cases are to be played in this manner, that you may avoid being shut up in your adversary's tables, and have the chance of throwing high doublets to win the hit.]

Two fours, two of them are to take your adversary's cinque-point in his tables ; and for the other two, two men are to be brought from the five placed in your adversary's tables.

Cinque-ace, play the cinque from the five men

placed in your adversary's tables, and play the ace from your adversary's ace-point.

Quatre-ace, play the quatre from the five men placed in your adversary's tables, and the ace from the men on your adversary's ace-point.

Deuce-ace, play the deuce from the five men placed in your adversary's tables, and the ace from your adversary's ace-point.

Hoyle gives the following example of a

BACK-GAME.

Suppose A to have two men upon his six-point in his own tables, three men upon his usual point in his outer table, two men upon the point where his five men are usually placed in his adversary's tables, five men upon his adversary's ace-point, and three men upon his adversary's quatre-point :

And suppose B to have two men upon his six-point in his own tables, three men upon his usual point in his outer table, two men upon the point where his five men are usually placed in his adversary's tables, five men upon his adversary's ace-point, and three men upon his adversary's trois-point :

Who has the fairest chance to win the hit ?

A has, because he is to play either an ace, or a deuce, from his adversary's ace-point, in order to make both these points as occasion offers ; and having the quatre-point in his adversary's tables, he may more easily bring those men away, if he finds it necessary, and he will also have a resting place by the conveniency of that point, which at all times in the game will give him an opportunity of running for the hit, or staying, if he thinks proper;—whereas B cannot so readily come from the trois-point in his adversary's tables.

A CASE OF CURIOSITY.

Let us suppose A and B place their men in the following manner for a hit :—

Suppose A to have three men upon his six-point in his own tables, three men upon the usual point in his outer table, and nine men upon his adversary's ace, deuce, and trois-points, three men to be placed upon each point; and suppose B's men to be placed in his own, and in his adversary's tables, in the same order and manner.

The result is, that the best player ought to win the hit; and the dice are to be thrown for, the situation being perfectly equal in A's and B's game.

If A throws first, let him endeavor to gain his adversary's cinque-point; when that is effected, let him lay as many blots as possible, to tempt B to hit him; for every time that B hits them will be in A's favor, because it puts B backward; and let A take up none of B's men for the same reason.

CRITICAL CASE FOR A BACK-GAME.

Let us suppose A plays the fore-game, and that all his men are placed in the usual manner :

For B's game let us suppose that 14 of his men are placed upon his adversary's ace-point, and 1 man upon his adversary's deuce-point, and that B is to throw :

Which game is likeliest to win the hit ?

A's is the best by 21 *for*, to 20 *against;* because, if B misses an ace to take his adversary's deuce-point, which is 25 to 11 against him, A is, in that case, to take up B's men in his tables, either singly, or to make points ; and if B secures either A's deuce or trois point, in that case A is to lay as many men down as possible, in order to be hit, that thereby he may get a Back-game.

When you are pretty well versed in the game of Backgammon, by practising this Back-game you will become a greater proficient in the game than by any other method, because it clearly demonstrates the whole power of the Back-game.

CALCULATION OF CHANCES.

In playing Backgammon, it is of course necessary that the amateur should know how many points he ought to throw upon the two dice, one throw with the other.

The following demonstration of the chances is

given by Hoyle, and adopted by all succeeding writers on the game, simply because the matter, being one of fact, cannot be altered or improved:—

On the two dice there are thirty-six chances.

In these thirty-six chances there are the following points, namely:—

	Points.
2 aces..	4
2 deuces.......................................	8
2 trois...	12
2 fours...	16
2 fives...	20
2 sixes...	25
6 and 5 twice..................................	22
6 and 4 twice..................................	20
6 and 3 twice..................................	18
6 and 2 twice..................................	16
6 and 1 twice..................................	14
5 and 4 twice..................................	18
5 and 3 twice..................................	16
5 and 2 twice..................................	14
5 and 1 twice..................................	12
4 and 3 twice..................................	14
4 and 2 twice..................................	12
4 and 1 twice..................................	10
3 and 2 twice..................................	10
3 and 1 twice..................................	8
2 and 1 twice..................................	6

Divided by 36)294(8
288
————
6

Thus we see that 294 divided by 36 gives 8 and a little more as the average throw with two dice. The chances upon two dice are :—

2 sixes	1
2 fives	1
2 fours	1
2 trois	1
2 deuces	1
*2 aces	1
6 and 5 twice	2
6 and 4 twice	2
6 and 3 twice	2
6 and 2 twice	2
*6 and 1 twice	2
5 and 4 twice	2
5 and 3 twice	2
5 and 2 twice	2
*5 and 1 twice	2
4 and 3 twice	2
4 and 2 twice	2
*4 and 1 twice	2
3 and 2 twice	2
*3 and 1 twice	2
*2 and 1 twice	2

36

To find out by this table what are the odds of being hit upon a certain or flat die, look in the table where thus * marked,

*2 aces	1
*6 and 1 twice	2
*5 and 1 twice	2

*4 and 1 twice... **2**

*3 and 1 twice... **2**

*2 and 1 twice... **2**

Total............... **11**

Which deducted from.. **36**

The remainder is...... **25**

By this it appears that it is twenty-five to eleven against hitting an ace upon a certain or flat die.

The like method may be taken with any other flat die, as with the ace.

What are the odds of entering a man upon one, two, three, four, or five points ?

					For.		Against.
To enter it upon	1 point	is	about		4	to	9
"	" 2 "		"		5	to	4
"	" 3 "		"		3	to	1
"	" 4 "		"		8	to	1
"	" 5 "		"		35	to	1

The odds against hitting with double dice are :—

				For.		Against.
To hit upon	7	is about	5	to	1
" "	8	"	5	to	1
" "	9	"	6	to	1
" "	10	"	11	to	1
" "	11	"	17	to	1
" "	12	"	36	to	1

To further explain how to make use of the table of 36 chances, when at a loss to find the odds of

6eing hit upon a certain or flat die, another example is added. By the following we find the odds of being hit upon a six :—

	Points.
2 sixes.	I
2 trois.	I
2 deuces.	I
6 and 5 twice.	2
6 and 4 twice.	2
6 and 3 twice.	2
6 and 2 twice.	2
6 and 1 twice.	2
5 and 1 twice.	2
4 and 2 twice.	2
	17

Deduct this 17 from 36—the number of chances upon two dice—and we have 19. From this table then, we find that it is 19 to 17 against being hit upon a 6.

The odds of 2 love is about 5 to 2
 " " 2 to 1 " 2 to 1
 " " 1 love " 3 to 2

Here, then, we have the game of Backgammon as played in the politest circles. I trust I have made the method of playing it plain to the comprehension of the reader.

DRAUGHTS.

CHAPTER I.

THE game of Draughts is decidedly scientific; and though perhaps somewhat less so than Chess, is equally amusing and equally an exercise for the mind. It is governed entirely by calculation, and he who, by study and practice, becomes a good player at it, has really effected something more; for he has schooled his intellect in a system of logical discipline, and accustomed himself to find recreation in a rational and interesting study—no slight ends, I take it. Chess is said to be more than four thousand years old; but Draughts boasts a yet more remote ancestry, if we may believe its historians. The game of Draughts is to Chess what Arithmetic is to Algebra. Antiquarians agree in giving precedence, in point of age, to Draughts, on the ground that, among the New Zealanders and other savage tribes, the game is generally known.

Some, however, assert that it is the offshoot of Chess. It is, they say, the Chess of ladies. There would appear to be some truth in the argument; for in nearly all the European languages, Draughts is called the Game of Ladies. With the French it is the "Jeu des Dames"; the Germans, "Damenspiel"; the Italians, "Il Giuco delle Dame"; the Portuguese, "O Jogo das Damas"; and so forth. In Gaelic there is but one word, "Taileasg," both for Chess and Draughts; and the Scotch call the Draught-board a "dam-brod," probably from the German "Damenbrett," or ladies' board.

We have no authoritative record that Draughts was much practiced in Europe till the middle of the sixteenth century. In 1668 a treatise upon it was published in Paris by M. Mallet, a professor of mathematics. Nearly a century later, Mr. William Payne, also a teacher of mathematics, published his celebrated "Introduction to the Game of Draughts" (London, 1756). In 1767 appeared "A Companion for the Draught-player," by W. Painter. Until 1800 no other work on the game was issued by English writers, but in that year Joshua Sturges published his well known and most able work, "The Guide to the Game of Draughts." J. Sinclair (Glasgow, 1832) was the next to issue a treatise on the game, and was the first of the Scottish school of writers and players who have done so much to popularize a scientific study of the pastime; then followed J. Drummond's first edition (Falkirk, 1838), and W. Hay (Stirling, 1838). In 1848 Mr. Anderson published, at Lanark, his first work, followed, in 1852, by his celebrated "Second Edition."

It is played, on a board exactly like a Chess-board, by two players. The board is placed so that a double corner is at the right hand of the player. The following is a representation of the

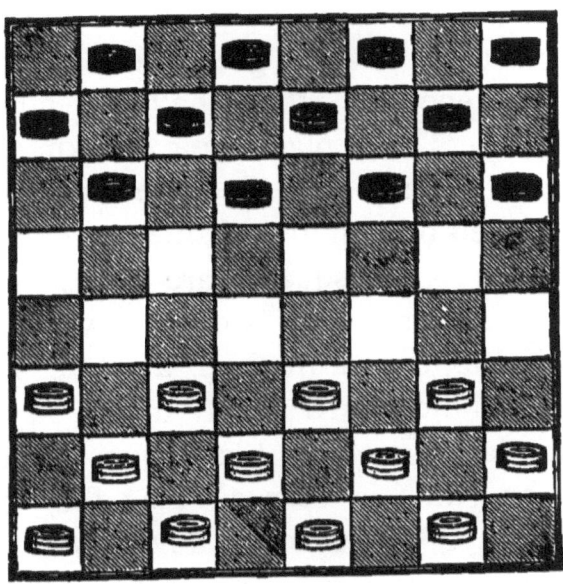

DRAUGHT-BOARD, WITH THE MEN ARRANGED
IN THEIR PROPER ORDER.

It is unimportant whether the players choose the black or the white squares, so that the double corner is at the right hand.

Each player has twelve men, which move in *diagonal lines*, and take by passing over the opponent on to the empty square beyond. A man enabled to pass on to the last row of his adversary's side becomes a King, which has the power of moving backwards as well as forwards. The game is over when one player succeeds in either taking all his adversary's men or in blocking them so that they cannot move.

The instructions of Edmond Hoyle are so plain and satisfactory, that I give them, despite the necessity of repeating what I have already stated.

"The players may place their men on either the black or white squares, but the whole of them must be placed on squares of one color only. In Scotland, the black squares are generally played on; in England, the play is on the white; consequently, in the former method, a white square in the corner of the board is left to the right hand, and by the latter mode a black one. The operation of the game is very simple; the 'men' are moved always diagonally, never sideways or straight forward, and only one square at a time. If one of the enemy's men stand in the way, no move can be effected, unless there be a vacant square beyond him, in which case he is leaped over; and being thus taken, is removed from the board. As the pieces can only be moved diagonally, and one square at a time, there can be no taking until the antagonists have moved their men into close quarters; and in pushing the pieces thus cautiously forward at the opening, consists the chief art of the game—the grand object being to hem-in the enemy in such a manner that he cannot move his men. When the men of either opponent have made their way to the opposite end of the board, either by taking or through an open path left by preceding moves, they receive increased power : they are then ' crowned,' which is performed by placing one of the enemy's captured men on the top of the piece which has penetrated to the enemy's first row of squares ; and thus 'crowned' the piece may be moved backwards as well as forwards—but still diagonally only, and one square at a time. To get a man ' crowned' is therefore of the first importance, as the more pieces either player has thus invested with the privilege of backward or forward movement, the greater are his chances of beating his adversary's men off the board and winning the game."

In brief, the men move one square at a time, and take in the direction in which they move, either right or left, by jumping over any adverse piece or pieces that may lie immediately in their path with a white square behind. Arrived at the last squares on the adversary's side, the men become Kings, and are crowned by placing one man on the top of the other. Kings take and move either forward or backward.

CHAPTER II.

THE MOVES, AND THE METHOD OF NOTATION.

FOR the convenience of noting the moves of the game, it has been agreed among modern players to number the white squares from 1 to 32 in the following manner :—

THE BOARD NUMBERED.

This system of numbering does not necessarily

take place on the board itself, but is rather employed for the purpose of enabling the players to note the moves on paper, and to play without seeing the board.

The moves of the pieces—we repeat ourselves, in order that the student may remember fully the preliminaries of the game—are all made in one direction—*diagonally forward, one square at a time.* A King, however, can move forward or backward at pleasure. All the pieces move on one colored square. Thus, if you play on the white you must keep on the white.

The pieces are captured by jumping over to the vacant square beyond, and not by assuming the place of the man taken, as in Chess ; the captured piece is then removed from the board.

On arriving at its eighth square on the opposite side of the board from which it started, the man is crowned, and becomes a King ; the operation of crowning is very simple—one piece being placed on the top of the other.

A man or King can take one or more men or Kings that may be *en prise ;* that is to say, if there be a vacant square beyond each piece captured.

The game is won by either taking all your adversary's men, or by blocking them in such a way as that they cannot move without being taken, or have no squares in which to move.

Each player moves alternately ; the first move in the game being usually determined by choice of color. It is common for black to play first, and to change the men with each game.

Let us now, in order to more fully show the *modus operandi,* play a short game, or, rather, part of one.

The players determine by lot which shall have the first move. After the first game, the first move is taken in rotation, it being usual for the first move to be made with the black, the board being turned for this purpose.

Black plays a man from square 11 to square 15 ; which White answers by playing a man from square 22 to 18. Black jumps over to square 22, takes the man, and removes it from the board ; and the game proceeds thus, the moves in which a piece is taken being marked by a star.*

The first moves were—

Black.	White.
11 to 15	22 to 18

Then

15 to 22*	25 to 18*
8 to 11	29 to 25
4 to 8	25 to 22
12 to 16	24 to 20

8 to 12	21 to 17

This move ought to lose White the game.

9 to 14	18 to 9*
5 to 21*	

You see that White loses two pieces for one, and has a bad position.

	28 to 24
3 to 8	32 to 28 (bad)
10 to 14	22 to 18
1 to 5	·18 to 9*
5 to 14*	26 to 22
6 to 10	31 to 26
10 to 15	22 to 17 ·
7 to 10	17 to 13
2 to 6	

This move stops White's advance to king.

	26 to 22
15 to 19	24 to 15*
10 to 26*	30 to 23*

Though this is only an exchange of two for two, Black is enabled presently to make a king.

14 to 17	22 to 18
21 to 25 .	18 to 15
11 to 18*	20 to 4*

Taking two pieces and making a king.

18 to 22	23 to 19
22 to 26	27 to 24
26 to 31	

Making a king, which speedily becomes effective.

	24 to 20 (A)
25 to 30	
becoming a king	20 to 16
30 to 27	16 to 11
27 to 24	19 to 15
24 to 19	

And Black wins the man and the game.

(A.) Suppose instead of playing 24 to 20, White plays 19 to 15, it will be found that he equally loses the game.

	19 to 15
31 to 27	24 to 20
17 to 22	15 to 11
22 to 25	11 to 7
25 to 29	
becoming a king	
	7 to 2
	also becoming a king.
6 to 10	2 to 6
10 to 15	6 to 10
15 to 18	28 to 24

And now, if White play carefully, he can draw the game, with two kings against two.

———

This system of notation will enable any one

thoroughly learning it to play a game without seeing the board. This is by no means difficult. I
have seen a player engage in half a dozen games
simultaneously without the board. In Draughts,
as well as in Chess, this is a mere effort of memory,
and is by no means necessary to good play.

CHAPTER III.

NAMES OF THE GAMES, OR OPENINGS, AND HOW FORMED.

1. The "Ayrshire Lassie," counting the play on both sides, is formed by the first four moves :—11-15, 24 20, 8-11, 28 24.

2. The "Bristol" is formed by the first three moves :—11-16, 24 20, 16-19. It was so named in compliment to the players of that city for services rendered to Mr. Anderson. Other authors, however, give the name "Bristol" to all games proceeding from Black's first move, 11-16.

3. The "Cross" is formed by the first two moves :—11-15, 23 18. It is so named because the second move is played across the direction of the first.

4. The "Defiance" is formed by the first four moves :—11-15, 23 19, 9-14, 27 23. It is so named because it defies or prevents the formation of the "Fife" game.

5. The "Double Corner" is so named from its first move—9-14—being from the one double corner toward the other. Although Anderson mentions the game in his list of the standard openings, he published no play upon it. Every variation in this edition, therefore, has an asterisk at it.

6. The "Dyke" is formed by the first three moves :—11-15, 22 17, 15-19. The name has probably arisen from the observed resemblance of many of the positions in this game to a "dyke" (*i. e.*, a fence or stone wall), for at various stages the pieces are frequently formed into straight lines.

7. The "Fife" is formed by the first five moves :—11-15, 23 19, 9-14, 22 17, 5-9. It has been so called since 1847, when Wyllie, hailing from Fifeshire, played it against Anderson.

8. The "Glasgow" is formed by the first five moves :— 11-15, 23 19, 8-11, 22 17, 11-16. It has been generally known by this name since Sinclair, of Glasgow, played it against Anderson at their match in Hamilton in 1828.

9. The "Laird and Lady" is formed by the first five moves : —11-15, 23 19, 8-11, 22 17, 9-13. It was so called from the fact of its having been the favorite of Laird and Lady Cather, who resided in Cambusnethan, Lanarkshire.

10. The "Maid of the Mill" is formed by the first five moves :—11-15, 22 17, 8-11, 17 13, 15-18. It was so named in compliment to a miller's daughter in Lanarkshire, who was an excellent player, and partial to this opening.

11. The "Old Fourteenth" is formed by the first five moves :—11-15, 23 19, 8-11, 22 17, 4-8. It was so named through being familiar to players as the 14th game in Sturges' original work.

12. The "Second Double Corner" is formed by the first two moves :—11-15, 24 19. Like the "Double Corner," it is so named because the first move of the *second* player is from the one double corner toward the other. This opening appeared in Anderson's first edition under the very inappropriate name of the "Invincible."

13. The "Single Corner" is formed by the first two moves : —11-15, 22 18. It is so named from the fact of each of these moves being played from one single corner toward the other.

14. The "Souter" is formed by the first five moves :—11-15, 23 19, 9-14, 22 17, 6-9. The game has been known by this

name amongst players in Scotland for many years, and was so named owing to its being the favorite of an old Paisley shoe-maker (*Scottice*, souter).

15. The "Whilter" is formed by the first five moves :— 11–15, 23 19, 9–14, 22 17, 7–11.   There was no play published on this opening previous to its appearance in Anderson's first edition.   "Whilter" or "Wholter" (in Scotch) signifying an overturning, or a change productive of confusion, is remarkably applicable to many of the unexpected changes which occur in this game.

16. The "Will o' the Wisp" is formed by the first three moves :—11–15, 23 19, 9–13.   It was so named by Mr. G. Wallace, of Glasgow, from the peculiarity of some of the variations, where the player finds to his loss he has been pursuing an *ignis fatuus*.

We need scarcely remark that the games formed by an *odd* number of moves refer to the first side, while those formed by an *even* number refer to the second.   For instance, if one says that he played the "Ayrshire Lassie," "Defiance," "Cross," "Second Double Corner," or "Single Corner" against his opponent, we at once understand that he played the *second* side of the games,

CHAPTER IV.

STANDARD LAWS OF THE GAME.

THE established rules of the game of Draughts are few, and easy to remember. If my readers will carefully follow the directions I now give them, they will soon become acquainted with all that the best players acknowledge as leading rules. The paragraphs within brackets are merely explanatory.

1. The Standard Board must be of light and dark squares, not less than fourteen and one-half inches nor more than sixteen inches across said squares.

2. The Standard Men, technically described as Black and White, must be light and dark (say Red and White or Black and White), turned, and round, not less than one and one-eighth inch, nor more than one and one-fourth inch in diameter.

3. The board must be placed so that the White double corner is at the right hand of the player.

[This is important, as all the games are given on this presumption. Otherwise, it is of no consequence on which colored squares you play.]

4. The first move of each game must be taken alternately by each player, whether the last be won or drawn.

[The usual plan is for the Black to move first. This is simply done by changing the men. The player who had Black in the first game will have taken White pieces, which he proceeds to arrange for the second game, and so on.]

5. Pointing over the board, or using any action to interrupt the opponent in having a full view of the game, is not allowed.

[There is no penalty for this practice ; but the fact that it is disagreeable and ungentlemanly, ought to be sufficient to deter any player.]

6. It is optional with the player either to allow his opponent to stand the huff, or to compel him to take the offered piece.

["Standing the huff" is when the player has a piece offered to him and he refuses to take it, but makes another move. His opponent then removes the man that should have played from the board, and makes his own move.]

7. If either player, when it is his turn to play, hesitate to make his move for more than five minutes, his opponent may call upon him either to move or resign the game. A delay of another minute in moving loses the game.

[This is the rule ; but it may, of course, be varied by consent of the players.]

8. Neither player is allowed to quit the room during the progress of a game without his opponent's consent.

9. In the losing, equally with the winning game, it is compulsory upon the player to take all the men he can legally take by the same move. On making a King, however, the latter must remain on his square till a move has been made on the opposite side.

10. When there is only *one way* of taking *one* or *more* pieces, "Time" shall be called at the end of One Minute ; and if the move be not completed on the expiry of another minute, the game shall be adjudged as lost through improper delay.

11. Either player is entitled, on giving intimation, to arrange

his own or his opponent's pieces properly on the squares. After the first move has been made, however, if either player touch or arrange any piece without giving intimation to his opponent, he shall be cautioned for the first offence, and shall forfeit the game for any subsequent act of the kind.

12. After the pieces have been arranged, if the person whose turn it is to play *touch* one, he must either play *it* or forfeit the game. When the piece is *not playable*, he is penalized according to the preceding law.

13. If *any part* of a playable piece be played over an angle of the square on which it is stationed, the play must be completed in *that direction.*

14. When taking, if a player remove one of his own pieces, *he* cannot replace it ; but his *opponent* can either play or insist on his replacing it.

15. When a small number of men only remain in the game, the player having the minority of pieces, may call upon his opponent to win in fifty moves, or declare the game drawn. With two Kings opposed to one, the game is declared drawn, unless it be won in, at most, twenty moves.

> [This, again, is a rule for expert players. With amateurs it is not well to act upon it with severity. With two men against one, however, it is always easy for the player with the superior number to drive his opponent into the double corner ; and, when he is there, to win the game in, at most, eight moves.]

16. All disputes are to be decided by the majority of the persons present.

17 A false move must be remedied, or the game is lost.

18. The player who refuses to abide by the rules, loses the game.

A FEW HINTS TO PLAYERS.

It is judicious to keep your men towards the centre of the board, in the form of a pyramid. Be careful to back up your advanced men so as not to leave a chance of your opponent taking two for one. A man on a side square is deprived of half his offensive power.

Be careful to look well over the board before making your move; but let not your caution descend to timidity. Resolve the consequences of every move before making it.

Never touch a man without moving it.

Avoid the inelegant act of pointing with your finger across the board. Determine on your move, and make it without hesitation.

Avoid conversation that is likely to be annoying or confusing to your adversary. If you prove the conqueror, endeavor to act the part of a noble one, and triumph not over a fallen enemy. Even when often defeated, let your loss act rather as a spur to increased care, watchfulness, and practice, than as a provocative of ill-blood.

He who abandons the game, loses it.

Keep your temper.

A correspondent writes :—" In playing with some friends of mine, I have often met with cases of *cowardly play ;* by which I mean their giving man for man, when they have more men than myself. Please state whether you consider it cowardly or not, and if there is a rule against so doing. It requires little science to play in that manner ; and if it is lawful to play so, I think it spoils the game ; but kindly enlighten me a little on this point."—It is not cowardly to give man for man when you are a piece a-head ; but it is considered the high game not to do so. There is no rule against the practice of " manning ; " and if there were, it could not be carried out, because in some situations it is almost impossible to win when you have advantage of a piece without reducing your adversary to a single man. Then you drive him into the double corner and beat him in a regular number of moves.

General rules for manning cannot well be given, seeing that each game necessarily differs in many important respects. The young player will do well, however, to remember that it is better to keep his men in the middle of the board than to play them to the side squares, when half their power is lost. The advice of Sturges, whose work is the foundation of all that has been written on the game since the beginning of the present century, may be safely followed. He says :—" When you have once gained an advantage in the number of pieces, increase the proportion by exchanges ; but in forcing them, take care not to damage your position. Accustom yourself to play slowly at first, and, if a beginner, play with those who agree to allow an unconditional time for the consideration of a difficult position. Never touch a man without moving it, and do not permit the loss of a few games to ruffle your temper, but rather let continued defeat act as an incentive to greater efforts both of study and practice. When one player is decidedly stronger than another, he should give odds, to make the game equally interesting to both. There must be a great disparity indeed if he can give a man, but it is very common to give one man in a rubber of three games, the superior player engaging to play one game with 11 men instead of 12. Another description of odds consists in giving the drawn games ; that is, the superior allows the weaker player to reckon as won, all games he draws. Never play with a better player without offering to take such odds as he may choose to give. If, on the other hand, you find yourself superior to your adversary, that you feel no interest in playing—offer him odds, and should he refuse, cease playing with him unless he will play for a stake ; the losing which, for a few games in succession, will soon bring him to his senses.

Follow the rules of the game rigorously, and compel your antagonist to do the same ; without which, Draughts are mere child's play. If you wish to improve, play with better players, in preference to such as you can beat; and take every opportunity of looking on when fine players are engaged. Never touch the squares of the board with your finger, as some do, from the supposition that it assists their powers of calculation ; and accustom yourself to play your move off when you have once made up your mind."

STANDING THE HUFF.

With many players, some uncertainty appears to exist on the subject of "Standing the Huff." There should be no misunderstanding on this point, as it is of importance that the player offering the piece should be allowed all the advantages arising from his skill and ingenuity.

The following, from the valuable treatise of Sturges, as revised by Walker in 1835, and admitted by all good players, sets the matter in a very clear light.

"In the case of standing the huff, it is optional on the part of the adversary, to take the capturing piece, whether man or King, or to compel you to take the piece or pieces of his, which you omitted by the huff. The necessity of this law is evident, when the young player is shown that it is not unusual to sacrifice two or three men in succession, for the power of making some decisive '*coup*.' Were this law different, the players might take the first man so offered, and on the second's being placed '*en prise*,' might refuse to capture, and thus, by quietly standing the huff, spoil the beauty of the game, which consists in brilliant re- sults arising from scientific calculation. It should be observed, however, that on the principle of 'touch and move,' the option ceases the moment the huffing party has so far made his election as to touch the piece he is entitled to remove.—After a player entitled to huff has moved without taking his adversary, he cannot remedy the omission, un- less his adversary should still neglect to take or to change the position of the piece concerned, and so leave the opportunity. It does not matter how long a piece has remained '*en prise*'; it may at any time either be huffed or the adversary be com- pelled to take it.—When several pieces are taken at one move, they must not be removed from the board until the capturing piece has arrived at its destination ; the opposite course may lead to dis- putes, especially in Polish draughts.—The act of huffing is not reckoned as a move ; 'a huff and a move' go together."

Thus it will be seen that the adversary must take the piece offered, if the player insists on his so doing. The usual plan is to offer the piece and say, "*Take that,*" after which the huff is not allowed among players of reputation.

WINNING WITH THREE KINGS TO TWO.

It has often been a question with players, whether, towards the end of a game, when one player was left with a man more than his opponent, it was altogether honorable to give man for man. Now, as there is nothing contrary to rule in this practice, so, I think, there can be nothing in it that can be said to be unfair. Indeed, it is sometimes almost impossible to finish the game without exchanging men. In some situations the player with two Kings can so move them as to render the winning of the game by his opponent with three Kings, impracticable. Obviously, therefore, the proper plan is, for the player with the superior force to reduce his adversary to a single King, drive him into the double corner, and win. This is very easy. Remembering the position of the board, with the white squares marked from 1 (at the left-hand upper corner) to 32 (the right-hand lower white square), we will suppose that Black has a single King in square 28; the

White then brings up his men so as to occupy the
squares 23 and 19.   He then moves—

Black.	White.
23 to 27	28 to 32
19 to 23	32 to 28
27 to 32	28 to 24
32 to 28	24 to 20
23 to 18	20 to 16
18 to 15	

Black then moves either to square 20 or 12.   In
either case White moves to square 11, when Black's
next move must be his last, as he must move into
a square commanded by one of his opponent's
pieces.   Thus it will be seen that the single man
can always be driven out of the double corner and
beaten in from seven to fifteen moves, no matter in
what part of the board the two Kings may happen
to be.   The grand principle is, to bring up your
men to the two squares in front of the double
corner with only one vacant square on each line
intervening.   From that position the superior force
can, as we have seen, win the game, in seven
moves, whether he has the move or not.

Now let me advise those of my friends who are
anxious to arrive at the honor of being considered
good players, to study the position of the numbered

board. They will thus become so familiar with the notation as soon to be able to play the printed games without even seeing the board.

TO KNOW WHEN YOU HAVE "THE MOVE."

The best and easiest method of ascertaining when you have the move has been stated by Mr. Martin, a player of great skill. To know when you have the move is a matter of considerable importance, especially towards the end of the game. In critical situations the possession of the move enables you to force the game and win. But if it happen that your own men are in a confined and cramped position, the knowledge as to which player will have the last move in the game is of little moment. This is a plan of discovering the player with the move :—Count all the pieces, both black and white, which stand on the columns—not the diagonals—which have a white square at the bottom. If the number be odd, and White has to play, White has the move : if the number be even, Black has the move.

Another method, which holds good, like the foregoing, with any number of men, is this :—If you desire to know whether any piece of yours has the move of any piece of your adversary's, you must examine the position of both. If you find a black square on the right angle under his man, you have the move. The most familiar example usually given by players is that quoted by Painter, who, in 1767, brought out a revised edition of Payne's *Treatise on Draughts*. And, by the way, Payne's book was probably founded on that of M. Mallett, a Parisian professor of mathematics, who a century earlier wrote a highly ingenious work on the game. Suppose you have a White man on square 30, and your opponent to have a Black man on square 3 ; in this position it will be seen that the right angle is in a black square between 31 and 32, directly under his man; consequently you have the move. Had your man been on square 29, the right angle would have been found on the black square between 30 and 31 ; or if it had been on square 31 the right angle would have fallen on the black square at the right-hand corner of the board, and the move would have been with your adversary.

There is yet another method. In order to know if you have the move, you must count the men and the squares. If the men are even and the squares odd, or if the squares are even and the men odd, you have the move ; with even squares and even men, or with odd squares and odd men, the move is with your antagonist. See this diagram :—

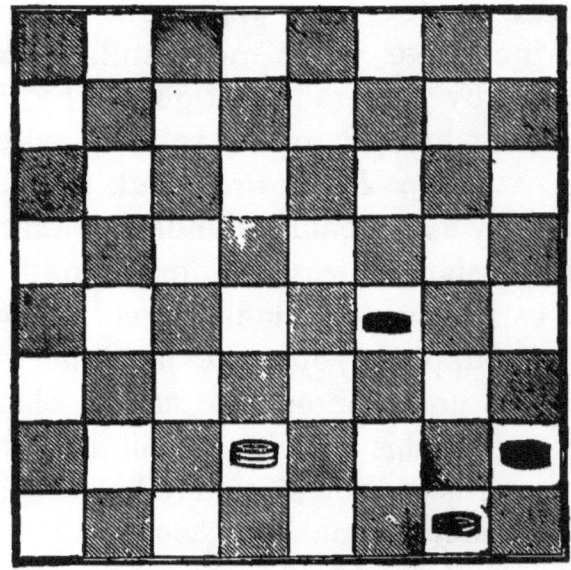

We reckon the square thus—From the White king on square 26 to the Black king on 28, the white squares are odd and the men even. From the White man on 32 to the Black man on 19 the squares are again odd ; then which has the move ? It will be seen that though the men are even, two to two, the squares are five in number—odd. In the giving of man for man it is very important to know with which player the move lies, as that often determines the game ; or in driving a man into a corner—as with three kings to two—you cannot give well the exchange without you have the move.

The player who begins the game certainly has

not the move, the men and the squares being both even ; but though the second player has the move, it is no manner of advantage to him at that period of the game. While the players continue to give man for man, the move belongs alternately to each, the one having it with an odd number of men—11, 9, 7, 5, 3, 1 ; the other with an even number—12, 10, 8, 6, 4, 2. Till some mistake be made by one or other of the players, the move cannot be forced.

———

The ultimate fate of the game cannot be affected by the first move if it is made towards the centre of the board ; but in the subsequent moves, if the game is not opened well, it must or ought to be lost. No bystander should be allowed to interfere, even if he sees a false move. Above all, the young player is recommended to use caution with promptitude, and decision with courtesy.

CHAPTER V.

ANDERSON'S THEORY OF THE MOVE AND ITS CHANGES PRACTICALLY EXPLAINED AND ILLUSTRATED.

WHEN the men are so situated that, in the ordinary course of the play, you can force your opponent's pieces into a confined position, you have what is technically termed "the Move." "The Move" in many positions wins the game, in others it enables a draw to be secured, while in some instances, from the peculiarity of the situation, the player having the move loses the game. Hence the importance of the knowledge which enables one to judge whether or not he should seek to gain "the Move."

The Move.

To have the move, signifies the occupying of that position on the board, which (in playing piece against piece, without regard to the others, till one square intervene between the pieces in each pair), will eventually cause the player who occupies that position to have the last play.

Calculation of the Move.

For convenience, the squares of the board are divided into two systems of four columns each. The columns of one system are those reckoned upward from Black's crown-head—that is, from the squares numbered 1, 2, 3, 4. The columns of the other system are those reckoned downward from White's crown-head—that is, from the squares numbered 29, 30, 31, 32.

Reckoning *upward*, the squares 1, 9, 17, 25—2, 10, 18, 26—3, 11, 19, 27—4, 12, 20, 28—form the columns of one system;

and reckoning *downward*, squares 29, 21, 13, 5—30, 22, 14, 6—31, 23, 15, 7—32, 24, 16, 8—form the columns of the other system. The following may more clearly show what is meant by two systems—the figures in ordinary type showing the columns of one system, and those in heavier type the columns of the other.

The columns of each system being situated alternately between those of the other, it is evident that one system is the reverse of the other.

When the two players have an equal number of pieces, it is obvious that the *total number* of pieces must always be even.

Now, as an *even number* can only be divided into *two even* or *two odd* numbers, it is clear that if the pieces be counted in each of the two systems separately, the numbers will in the two cases be both even or both odd.

In the course of the play each move will be out of one system into the other, and will therefore make one system count one more, and the other one less; so that if both systems were before odd, they will now be both even, and after another move they will again be both odd, and so on alternately, according to the player whose turn it is to play.

To know if you have the move WHEN IT IS YOUR TURN TO PLAY, *apply the following rules :—*

RULE I.—Add together all the pieces, both Black and White, in either system of squares, and if their sum is odd you have the move ; but if even, your opponent has the move.

As an illustration, take the following position :—

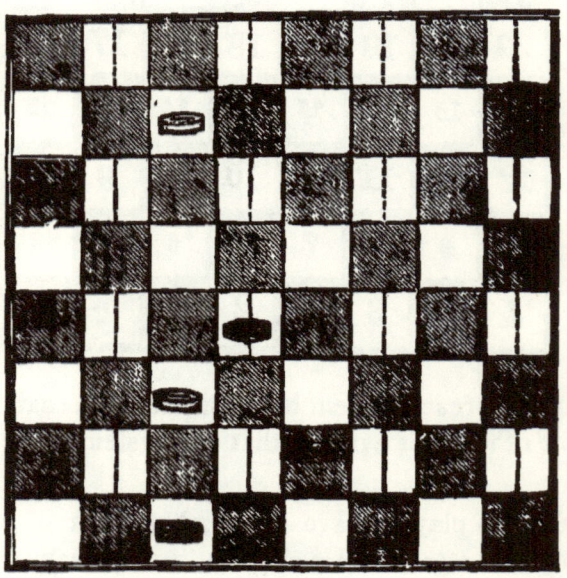

You play Black, and have the move, because either system contains an odd number of pieces ; one contains one, the other three. (To aid the beginner in mastering the idea of the two systems into which the board is divided, we have distinguished the one system from the other by a series of dots.)

Abbreviation of the Rule.

Add together all the *single pieces* and all the *single vacant squares* on the rows of either system, and if their sum is odd, you have the move : but if even, you have not.

Let it be observed that you will find the *single pieces* only on such *rows* of the set as contains one piece ; and the *single vacant squares* only on such as contain three pieces. You omit all rows of the set which contain two or four pieces, because an even number does not affect the result. In using this shortened form of the rule, you will never count more than ONE on any given row ; and THREE will be the greatest number in the whole set when you have the move, and FOUR when you have not.

To have the move is often an advantage, though to have it in some cases may occasion the loss of the game.

As an illustration, take the following position :—

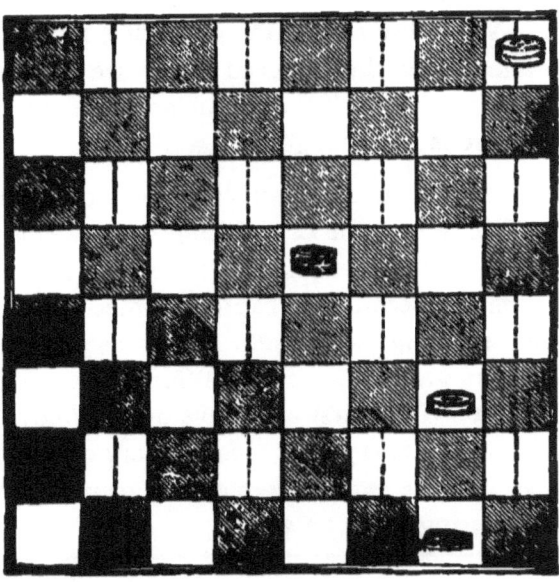

You play White first, and have the move, but lose the game, through Black forcing your man on 9 into 5—a confined position. The Black king has then the move on your king, though you have the move if all the pieces are counted.

An exchange usually alters the move ; consequently, when you wish to obtain the move, make such an exchange as will alter it.

Take the following position as an illustration :—Place Black men on 13 and 17, and White men on 26 and 30. You play Black and have not the move ; but play 17–22, White takes 26 17, you retake by 13–22, and gain the move.

In every single exchange of one for one, when only one of the capturing pieces remains on the board, the move is changed.

To find what kind of exchanges do, or do not change the move, apply the following rules :—

RULE II.—When the sum of the capturing pieces is even and in reverse systems, and the captured pieces are odd on each side, the move is changed ; but if the capturing pieces are in the same system, the move is not changed.*

Place the following as an illustration :—Black man on 11 and king on 26 ; White man on 22 and king on 7. You play White first and have not the move ; take 7 16, Black takes 26–17, and you gain the move, because the capturing piece on 7 is in reverse system to the capturing piece on 26. Place also the following :— Black man on 15 and king on 26 ; White man on 22 and king on 10. You play White first and have not the move. Take 10 19, and Black takes 26–17, and this exchange does not change the move, because the capturing piece on 10 is in the same system as the capturing piece on 26.

---

* You must apply the rules at the squares the pieces capture and are captured from.

Rule III.—When the sum of the capturing pieces is even and the captured pieces are even on each side, the move is not changed.

Rule IV.—When the sum of the capturing pieces is odd and the captured pieces are even in each system, the move is changed ; but if the captured pieces are odd the move is not changed.

As a summary of the illustrations of the exchanges which do or do not change the move, the following will be found of universal application in the most complex positions :—

Rule V.—Add together *all* of the capturing pieces in both systems, and if they are the same as the captured pieces in each system (that is, both odd or both even), the move is not changed; but if they are reverse to each other (one odd and the other even), the move is changed.

THE LOSING GAME.

A very pleasing variety in Draughts is made by playing what is called the Losing Game. He who first *loses* all his men *wins* the game. This losing your men is not so easy as might at first sight appear. The secret of success lies, however, in a very simple series of moves. What you have to do is, to open your game by giving piece for piece for the first three or four moves, and then open your back squares, and leave spaces between them and the advanced pieces, so as to enable you at a favorable opportunity to give two men for one.

Having lost a man more than your opponent, be careful to retain that advantage by giving man for man. But you must not be too anxious to crown your men, or to pass the squares protected by your opponent's pieces. If you do, he will presently regain his loss, and perhaps turn the tables upon you. Sometimes it will happen that with a single King you can compel your adversary to give up piece after piece till you find yourself able to offer yourself as a sacrifice and win. In the Losing game you must take the piece offered, and he who refuses it loses the game, of course. There is no such thing as standing the huff in the Losing Game.

In the Losing Game it is well to gain the side squares ; as, when your opponent advances, as he must after a while, you are enabled to offer your men with the certainty of losing them. All pieces that can be taken must be taken. Great care is necessary in order to keep the move, for the player who has it ought always to win.

CHAPTER VI.

ELEMENTARY POSITIONS.

FIRST POSITION.

WHITE.

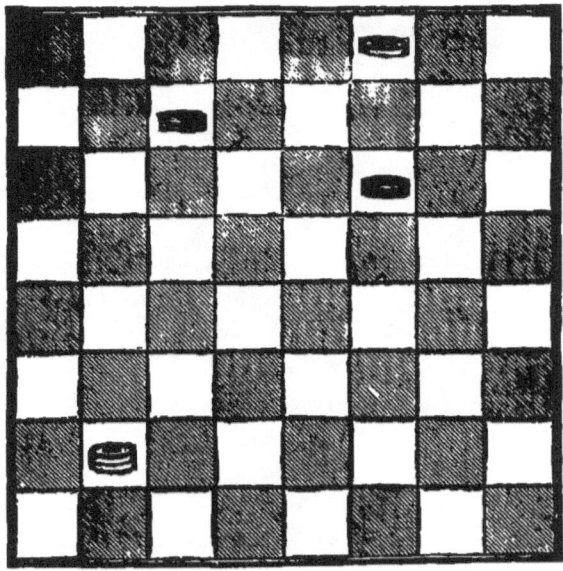

BLACK.

Black to play and win.

			1	5 9	2
27–32	10– 6	15–18		10–15	
8 11	5 1	17 13		2– 9 5	9 14
32–27	14–10	18–15	30 25	15–18	1– 5
11 7	1 5	9 14	23–18	5 9	21 17
27–23	6– 1	1– 5	10 6	1– 5	5– 1
7 10	5 9	14 17	18–14	9 6	17 13
22–26	1– 5	8–15–10	6 1	18–15	1– 5
1–10 6	9 13	17 22	26–30	21 17	14 17
26–31	10–14	10–14	25 21	5– 1	15–10
6 9	13 9	22 25	30 25	6 9	
31–26	14–18	5 1	1 5	15–18	Same as
9 6	9 6	25 22	25 22	9 5	trunk at s.
26–22	18–15	1– 6	5 1	18–22	
6 10	30 25	22 25	22–18	17 14	B. wins.
23–18	15–18	6–10	1 5	1– 6	
10 6	6 10	25 22	18 15	5 1	
18–14	5– 1	10 15	5 1	6– 2	
6 1	25 21	22 25	15–10	1 5	
22–18	1– 5	15 18	1 5	22–17	
1 6	10 6	25 21	10 6	14 9	
18–15	18–15	18–22	5 1	17–14	
6 1	21 17	B. wins.	14–10	B. wins.	
15–10	5 1		1 5		
1 5	6 9		6 1		

DRAUGHTS.

SECOND POSITION.

WHITE.

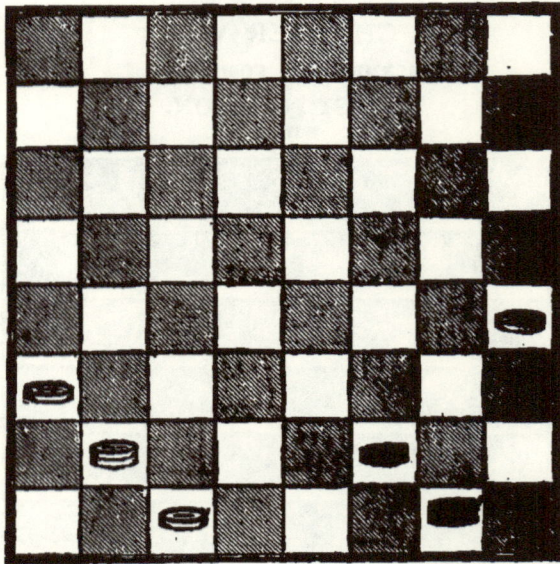

BLACK.

Black to play and win.

1- 5	27-31	27-24	18-14
8 11	32 28	32 28	4 8
5- 9	31-27	24-19	9- 1
11 15	28 32	28 32	8 11
9-14	27-23	19-15	14- 9
15 11	32 28	32 28	13 6
14-18	23-18	15-10	1-10
11 16	28 23	28 24	11 16
18-15	18-14	10- 6	10-15
16 20	24 19	24 19	16 20
15-11	6-10	14-10	15-19
20 24	19 23	19 24	
3- 7	10-15	10-15	B. wins
24 19	23 27	24 28	
7-10	15-19	15-19	
19 23	27 32	28 32	
10-15	19-24	19-24	
23 27	32 28	32 28	
15-19	24-27	11-16	
27 32	28 24	28 19	
19-24	27-32	16-23	
32 28	24 28	12 8	
24-27	32-27	23-18	
28 32	28 32	8 4	

THIRD POSITION.

WHITE.

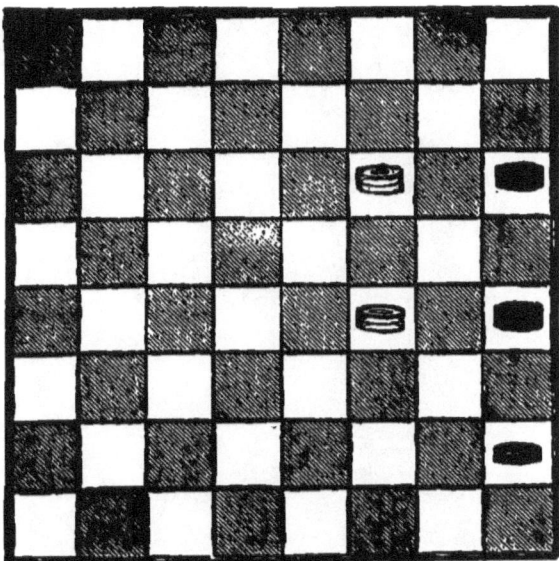

BLACK.

Black to play and win.

		1	2	3	4
13- 9	27-23.				
22 18	3-22 25				
9- 6	2- 7	14 18	14 17	14 !0	22 18
18 22	25 22	5- 9	5- 9	23-19	23-27
6- 1	7-11	18 23	A-17 21	10 14	18 22
1-22 18	4-22 25	1- 6	9-14	19-15	11-15
21-25	11-15	23 26	18 9	14 9	22 26
2-18 15	25 22	6-10	1- 5	15-10	27-24
1- 6	23-27	26 30	21 30	B. wins.	26 22
14 17	22 26	10-15	5-14		24-20
6- 2	27-24	30 26	30 26		22 26
17 14	24-20	15-19	14-18		20-16
25-22	22 26	26 30	B. wins.		26 22
15 10	20-16	19-23			16-12
22-26	26 22	22 26	A		B. wins.
14 18	16-12	23-18	18 15		
5- 9	22 26	26 31	25-21		
10 6	12- 8	18-22	17 22		
9-13	26 22	31 27	21-17		
6 10	8- 3	21-17	22 6		
26-31	14 9	27 31	1-19		
10 14	15-10	9-14	B. wins.		
31-27	B. wins.	B. wins.			
18 22					

FOURTH POSITION.

WHITE.

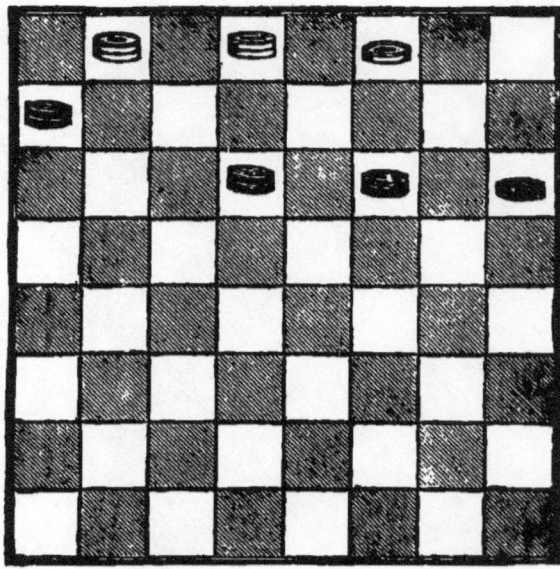

BLACK.

Black to play and win.   White to play and draw.

B. to play.	W. to play.
28–24	31 27
32 28	23–19
24–20	27 31
28 32	19–24
22–18	32 27
31 27	24–20
23–19	27 32
27 31	22–18
19–24	31 27
32 27	28–24
24–28	27 31
27 32	18–23
18–22	31 26
31 27	
22–26	Drawn.
30 23	
28–24	
B. wins.	

CHAPTER VII.

ILLUSTRATIVE GAMES.

In the following games the notation shown on page 13 is observed. Of course it will be understood that the moves are not always the very best that could be made; otherwise the first player would always be the winner. But by the study of them the young player will soon discover the reasons for the several combinations displayed. Each game is capable of many variations; and each variation in some measure alters the result. In Draughts, as in Chess, the different styles of opening the games lead to different styles of play.

GAME I.

Black.	White.
11 to 15	22 to 27
8 to 11	17 to 13
4 to 8	23 to 19
15 to 18	24 to 20
11 to 15	28 to 24
8 to 11	26 to 23
9 to 14	31 to 26

Black.	White.
6 to 9	13 to 6
2 to 9	26 to 22
9 to 13	32 to 28*
1 to 6	21 to 17
14 to 21	23 to 4
10 to 26	19 to 1
13 to 17	30 to 23
21 to 30	1 to 6
3 to 8	6 to 2
7 to 10	23 to 19
10 to 14	

And the game is drawn. The move of White at which the star is placed, was bad, and all he could hope to do, was to draw the game. If, instead of playing 32 to 28, he had moved from 20 to 16, he would have won; thus—

	20 to 16
11 to 20	22 to 17
13 to 22	21 to 17
14 to 21	23 to 14
10 to 17	25 to 2
1 to 6	2 to 9
5 to 14	19 to 15
3 to 8	24 to 19

Of course it will be understood that the moves given are not absolutely necessary in order to win

the game. Try variations from the 4th and 5th
moves of the Black, and you will produce a different result. If, for instance, Black plays as his 4th
move, instead of 15 to 18—

9 to 14 ;

White replies by playing—

27 to 23

And the game ought to be either drawn, or won
by the Black. But if, as his 5th move, he plays
10 to 14 instead of 11 to 15, the chances are in
favor of his winning ; certainly of making a draw.

Game II.

Black.	White.
11 to 15	22 to 18
15 to 22	25 to 18
8 to 11	29 to 25
4 to 8	25 to 22
12 to 16	24 to 20
10 to 15	27 to 24†
16 to 19	23 to 16
15 to 19	24 to 15
9 to 14	18 to 9
11 to 25	32 to 27
5 to 14	27 to 23
6 to 10	16 to 12
8 to 11	28 to 24

Black.	White.
25 to 29	30 to 25
29 to 22	26 to 17
11 to 15	20 to 16
15 to 18	24 to 20
18 to 27	31 to 24
14 to 18	16 to 11
7 to 16	20 to 11
18 to 23	11 to 8
23 to 27	8 to 4
27 to 31	4 to 8
31 to 27	24 to 20
27 to 23	8 to 11
23 to 18	11 to 8†
18 to 15 and wins.	

The moves marked with a dagger are those which lost White the game.

GAME III.

Black.	White.
11 to 15	22 to 17
8 to 11	23 to 19
4 to 8	25 to 22
9 to 13	17 to 14
10 to 17	19 to 10
7 to 14	29 to 25
3 to 7	27 to 23

Black.	White.
11 to 16A	31 to 27
8 to 11B	22 to 18
16 to 20	18 to 9
5 to 14	23 to 19
11 to 16	19 to 15
7 to 10	25 to 22
10 to 19	24 to 15
14 to 18	21 to 14

Drawn Game.

VARIATION A.

6 to 10	24 to 20
1 to 6	28 to 24
6 to 9	24 to 19
2 to 6	32 to 28
14 to 18	22 to 15
11 to 27	31 to 24
10 to 14	25 to 22
7 to 11	30 to 25
14 to 18	22 to 15
11 to 18	Drawn Game.

VARIATION B.

6 to 10	22 to 18
8 to 11	18 to 9
5 to 14	24 to 20

Black.	White.
11 to 15	20 to 11
7 to 16	25 to 22
16 to 19	23 to 16
12 to 19	27 to 23
1 to 6	23 to 16
14 to 18	21 to 7
18 to 25	30 to 21
2 to 20	Drawn Game.

The following game, with the variations, will give the young player a better insight into the art and mystery of Draughts than any merely verbal instructions.

GAME IV.

Black.	White.
11 to 15	22 to 17
8 to 11	23 to 19
4 to 8	25 to 22
9 to 13	17 to 14
10 to 17	19 to 10
7 to 14	29 to 25
2 to 7	27 to 23
11 to 16 A	22 to 18
6 to 10	18 to 9
5 to 14	24 to 20
16 to 19 B	23 to 16

Black.	White.
12 to 19	32 to 27
1 to 6	27 to 23
8 to 12	23 to 16
12 to 19	31 to 27
14 to 18	21 to 14C
10 to 17	25 to 22
18 to 25	Drawn Game.

VARIATION A.

11 to 15	31 to 27
8 to 11	24 to 20
15 to 19	23 to 16
12 to 19	27 to 23
3 to 8	23 to 16
8 to 12	32 to 27
12 to 19	27 to 23
11 to 15	23 to 16
15 to 19	16 to 11
7 to 16	Drawn Game.

VARIATION B.

8 to 11	28 to 24
10 to 15	23 to 19
16 to 23	26 to 10
11 to 15	30 to 26
7 to 11	26 to 23

Black.	White.
15 to 18	31 to 26
18 to 27	32 to 23
11 to 15	25 to 22
White wins.	

Variation C.

10 to 15	25 to 22
6 to 10	27 to 23
19 to 24	28 to 19
15 to 24	20 to 16
10 to 15	16 to 12
7 to 10	23 to 18
14 to 23	21 to 7
3 to 10	26 to 19
24 to 27	12 to 8
15 to 24	22 to 18
27 to 31	8 to 3
31 to 27	3 to 7
27 to 23	7 to 14
13 to 27	14 to 21
23 to 14	Drawn Game.

Game V.

22 to 17	11 to 15
23 to 19	8 to 11
25 to 22	9 to 13
17 to 14	10 to 17

Black.	White.
19 to 10	7 to 14
29 to 25	2 to 7
27 to 23	6 to 10 A
31 to 27	4 to 8
24 to 20	12 to 16 B
27 to 24	8 to 12
24 to 19	5 to 9 C
19 to 15	10 to 19
23 to 18	14 to 23
21 to 5	7 to 10
25 to 21	10 to 15
28 to 24	19 to 28
26 to 10	16 to 19
21 to 17	Drawn Game.

VARIATION A.

11 to 16	31 to 27
16 to 20	23 to 18
14 to 23	21 to 14
6 to 9	27 to 18
20 to 27	32 to 23
4 to 8	23 to 19
8 to 11	28 to 24
11 to 16	24 to 20
16 to 23	26 to 19
1 to 6	25 to 21
6 to 10	21 to 17

Black.	White.
7 to 11	14 to 7
3 to 10	19 to 16
12 to 19	17 to 14
10 to 26	Drawn Game.

VARIATION B.

10 to 15	23 to 18
14 to 23	21 to 14
7 to 10	27 to 18
10 to 17	32 to 27
12 to 16	27 to 23
8 to 12	28 to 24
5 to 9	23 to 19
16 to 23	26 to 10
17 to 26	30 to 23
13 to 17	23 to 19
17 to 22	25 to 21
22 to 26	21 to 17
9 to 13	17 to 14
26 to 30	19 to 15
30 to 26	15 to 8
26 to 22	14 to 9
22 to 6	9 to 2

Drawn Game.

VARIATION C.

3 to 8	32 to 27
5 to 9	22 to 18

Black.	White.
17 to 22	26 to 17
13 to 29	18 to 15
11 to 18	20 to 2
8 to 11	21 to 17
14 to 21 ·	23 to 7
11 to 16	Drawn Game.

GAME VI.

22 to 18	10 to 14
24 to 19	11 to 16
27 to 24	8 to 11
25 to 22	16 to 20
31 to 27	4 to 8
29 to 25	11 to 16 A
19 to 15	7 to 11
22 to 17	16 to 19
17 to 10	2 to 7
23 to 16	12 to 19
21 to 17	7 to 23
27 to 18	20 to 27
32 to 7	

White Wins, after several more moves, which
I leave the reader to play out for himself.

VARIATION A.

9 to 13	18 to 9
5 to 14	22 to 18
6 to 9	19 to 16

Black.	White.
12 to 19	24 to 15
7 to 10	15 to 6
1 to 10	23 to 19
14 to 23	27 to 18
20 to 24	26 to 22
10 to 15	19 to 10
2 to 7	28 to 19
7 to 23	19 to 15
11 to 18	22 to 15
8 to 11	15 to 8
3 to 12	25 to 28
2 to 16	22 to 18

And the game is drawn.

The following games are taken from Sturges. Supposing that Black plays first, White follows; and each plays moves alternately. In order to save space, the distinction between the White men and the Black has been omitted. But amateurs will as easily follow this as the other plan.

GAME VII.

11 to 15	25 to 18	12 to 16
24 to 20	4 to 8	21 to 17
8 to 11	29 to 25	7 to 10 Var.
22 to 18	10 to 15	17 to 13
15 to 22	25 to 22	8 to 12

28 to 24	24 to 20	2 to 11
9 to 14	18 to 22	26 to 10
18 to 9 .	27 to 24	6 to 15
5 to 14	22 to 26	28 to 24
23 to 19	19 to 15	5 to 9
16 to 23	12.to 19	27 to 23
26 to 19	13 to 9	1 to 6
3 to 8	6 to 22	31 to 26
31 to 26	15 to 6	6 to 10
15 to 18	1 to 10	32 to 28
22 to 15	24 to 6	3 to 7
11 to 18	Drawn.	23 to 19
32 to 28		W. wins.
2 to 7	Var.	
30 to 25	9 to 13	A.
7 to 11	17 to 14	12 to 19
25 to 21	16 to 19	27 to 23
18 to 22	23 to 16	7 to 14
26 to 17	8 to 12	23 to 7
11 to 25	14 to 10	W. wins.
20 to 16	7 to 23 A.	
15 to 18	16 to 7	

GAME VIII.

11 to 15	8 to 11	12 to 16
22 to 18	29 to 25	24 to 19
15 to 22	4 to 8	16 to 20
25 to 18	25 to 22	28 to 24 Var. A.

8 to 12	20 to 27	23 to 16
32 to 28	17 to 14	9 to 14
10 to 15	27 to 31	18 to 9
19 to 10	21 to 17	5 to 14
7 to 14	31 to 26	16 to 12
30 to 25	25 to 21	11 to 15
11 to 16	26 to 22	27 to 23
18 to 15	17 to 13	6 to 10
3 to 8	22 to 17	31 to 27
22 to 17	14 to 10	8 to 11
14 to 18	17 to 14	22 to 17
23 to 14	10 to 7	15 to 18
9 to 18	18 to 23	30 to 25
26 to 23	7 to 3	2 to 6
6 to 9	23 to 27	23 to 19
23 to 14	3 to 7	11 to 15
9 to 18	14 to 18	28 to 24
5 to 10	7 to 11	6 to 9
8 to 11	27 to 31	17 to 13
10 to 7	11 to 16	1 to 6
11 to 15	31 to 27	26 to 22
7 to 3	16 to 20	7 to 11
2 to 7	18 to 22	19 to 16
3 to 19	B. wins.	3 to 7
16 to 32		24 to 19
24 to 19	Var. A.	15 to 31
32 to 27	19 to 15	22 to 8
31 to 24	10 to 19	W. wins.

GAME IX.

22 to 18	15 to 24	1 to 6
11 to 15	28 to 19	30 to 25
18 to 11	1 to 6	6 to 10
8 to 15	30 to 26	25 to 21
25 to 22	3 to 8	10 to 17
4 to 8	26 to 23	21 to 14
29 to 25	8 to 11	7 to 10
8 to 11	23 to 18	14 to 7
23 to 18	11 to 16	3 to 10
9 to 13 Var.	27 to 23	32 to 28
18 to 14	16 to 20	10 to 14
10 to 17	31 to 27	26 to 22
21 to 14	6 to 9	14 to 17
6 to 10	18 to 15	19 to 15
25 to 21	9 to 18	Drawn.
10 to 17	23 to 14	
21 to 14	12 to 16	Var.
2 to 6	19 to 12	12 to 16
24 to 19	10 to 19	18 to 14 C.
25 to 14	12 to 8	10 to 17
28 to 19	Drawn.	22 to 13
6 to 10 A.		16 to 20 B.
22 to 17	A.	21 to 17
13 to 22	11 to 16	7 to 10
26 to 17	27 to 23	26 to 23
11 to 15	6 to 9	9 to 14
32 to 28	22 to 18	25 to 21

15 to 18	25 to 22	22 to 25
30 to 25	14 to 18	31 to 26
10 to 15	22 to 17	Drawn.
17 to 10	1 to 6	
18 to 22	32 to 27	C.
25 to 18	19 to 23	24 to 20
15 to 22	26 to 19	16 to 19
23 to 19	18 to 23	27 to 23 D.
6 to 15	27 to 18	9 to 13
19 to 10	15 to 22	B. wins.
22 to 25	17 to 14	
24 to 19	10 to 17	D.
2 to 7	21 to 14	27 to 24
Drawn.	6 to 10	10 to 14
	14 to 9	20 to 16
B.	5 to 14	14 to 23
9 to 14	13 to 9	31 to 27
24 to 20	14 to 17	11 to 20
6 to 10	9 to 5	27 to 11
27 to 24	17 to 21	7 to 16
16 to 19	5 to 1	24 to 15
		Drawn.

Game X.

22 to 18	21 to 17	17 to 13	25 to 22
11 to 15	4 to 8	9 to 14	14 to 17
18 to 11	23 to 19	27 to 23	29 to 25
8 to 15	8 to 11	5 to 9	17 to 21

22 to 17	17 to 10	3 to 9	20 to 11
11 to 16	6 to 24	16 to 19	7 to 16
25 to 22	13 to 6	23 to 16	1 to 5
7 to 11	1 to 10	12 to 19	16 to 20
24 to 20	22 to 17	9 to 5	5 to 9
15 to 24	24 to 28	19 to 24	24 to 27
28 to 19	17 to 13	5 to 1	Drawn.
10 to 14	3 to 7	11 to 16	

Game XI.

22 to 18	23 to 18	29 to 22
11 to 15	11 to 16	14 to 18
18 to 11	27 to 23 A.	23 to 14
8 to 15	16 to 20	6 to 10
21 to 17	32 to 27	15 to 6
4 to 8	10 to 14 Var.	2 to 25
23 to 19	17 to 10	19 to 15
8 to 11	7 to 14	25 to 30
17 to 13	18 to 9	27 to 23
9 to 14	5 to 14	20 to 27
25 to 21	13 to 9	31 to 24
14 to 18	6 to 13	30 to 26
26 to 23	19 to 15	23 to 18
18 to 22	1 to 6	26 to 22
30 to 26	24 to 19	18 to 14
15 to 18	3 to 7	12 to 16
26 to 17	28 to 24	16 to 11
18 to 22	22 to 25	Drawn.

A.

18 to 14	18 to 15	11 to 2
16 to 23	7 to 11	27 to 31
27 to 18	23 to 18	2 to 9
10 to 15	11 to 16	5 to 23
18 to 11	27 to 23	17 to 14
7 to 16	20 to 27	10 to 17
13 to 9	31 to 24	21 to 14
6 to 13	16 to 20	31 to 26
32 to 27	15 to 11	14 to 10
Drawn.	8 to 15	22 to 25
	18 to 11	29 to 22
Var.	20 to 27	26 to 17
3 to 8	23 to 18	B. wins.
	2 to 7	

Game XII.

22 to 18	14 to 18	18 to 15
11 to 15	26 to 23	19 to 23
18 to 11	18 to 22	15 to 11
8 to 15	23 to 18 Var.	10 to 14
21 to 17	11 to 16	11 to 8
4 to 8	18 to 11	22 to 26
23 to 19	16 to 23	31 to 22
8 to 11	27 to 18	14 to 17
17 to 13	7 to 16	21 to 14
9 to 14	24 to 20	6 to 9
25 to 21	16 to 19	13 to 6

1 to 26	5 to 14	31 to 27
8 to 4	32 to 27	6 to 10
Drawn.	14 to 18	27 to 23
	30 to 25	18 to 14
Var.	12 to 16	23 to 19
21 to 17	31 to 26	14 to 9
5 to 9	22 to 31	11 to 15
23 to 18	25 to 22	20 to 16
10 to 14	18 to 25	19 to 12
17 to 10	29 to 22	10 to 19
7 to 23	31 to 24	12 to 8
19 to 10	28 to 10	9 to 6
6 to 15	16 to 19	8 to 11
13 to 6	22 to 18	6 to 2
2 to 9	19 to 23	11 to 8
27 to 18	10 to 6	19 to 23
1 to 5	23 to 26	8 to 11
24 to 20	6 to 2	23 to 18
9 to 14	26 to 31	11 to 16
18 to 9	2 to 6	Drawn.

GAME XIII.

11 to 15	17 to 14 Var.	6 to 9
22 to 17	10 to 17	26 to 23
5 to 18	21 to 14	3 to 8
3 to 14	8 to 11	23 to 19
9 to 18	24 to 20	18 to 22

25 to 18	4 to 8	2 to 7A.
11 to 16	30 to 26	8 to 3
20 to 11	8 to 11	7 to 11
8 to 22	26 to 22	3 to 7
30 to 25	3 to 8	27 to 23
9 to 18	32 to 28	Drawn.
27 to 23	7 to 10	
18 to 27	24 to 19	A.
25 to 18	15 to 24	2 to 7
5 to 9	28 to 19	22 to 15
32 to 23	11 to 15	11 to 18
4 to 8	27 to 24	31 to 26
29 to 25	18 to 27	8 to 11
12 to 16	13 to 9	19 to 16
19 to 3	6 to 13	12 to 19
2 to 6	22 to 17	23 to 16
3 to 10	13 to 22	14 to 17
6 to 29	25 to 4	21 to 14
Drawn.	27 to 32	10 to 17
	4 to 8	16 to 12
Var.	32 to 27	11 to 15
17 to 13	29 to 25	12 to 8
8 to 11	5 to 9	17 to 21
26 to 23	25 to 22	25 to 22
10 to 14	9 to 13	18 to 25
24 to 20	8 to 11	Drawn.
11 to 15	1 to 5	
28 to 24	11 to 8	

Game XIV.

22 to 18	4 to 8	21 to 17	16 to 23
11 to 16	22 to 17	1 to 6	31 to 26
25 to 22	7 to 10	17 to 13	7 to 10
10 to 14	25 to 22	6 to 7	26 to 19
29 to 25	10 to 19	28 to 24	11 to 16
16 to 20	17 to 10	12 to 16	18 to 11
24 to 19	6 to 15	26 to 23	16 to 23
8 to 11	23 to 7	8 to 12	27 to 18
19 to 15	2 to 11	23 to 19	W. wins.

Game XV.

11 to 15	13 to 6	5 to 14
22 to 17	2 to 9	19 to 15
8 to 11	26 to 22	3 to 8
17 to 13	9 to 13B.	24 to 19
4 to 8	20 to 16	W. wins.
23 to 19	11 to 20	
15 to 18	22 to 17	A.
24 to 20	13 to 22	17 to 22
11 to 15	21 to 17	19 to 15
28 to 24	14 to 21	21 to 25
8 to 11	23 to 14	30 to 31
26 to 23	10 to 17	22 to 26
9 to 14	25 to 2	15 to 10
31 to 26	1 to 6A.	26 to 31
6 to 9	2 to 9	29 to 25

12 to 16	7 to 2	32 to 28
25 to 22	20 to 24	6 to 9
16 to 19	22 to 18	B wins.
24 to 15	11 to 16	
31 to 24	21 to 17	C.
15 to 11	W. wins.	32 to 28
24 to 19		9 to 13
11 to 7	B.	20 to 16
19 to 15	1 to 6	11 to 20
2 to 6	30 to 26C.	Drawn.
15 to 11	9 to 13	

Game XVI.

11 to 15	14 to 17	7 to 11
22 to 17	21 to 14	14 to 7
8 to 11	10 to 17	3 to 10
17 to 13	23 to 14	9 to 6
4 to 8	6 to 10	2 to 9
23 to 19	25 to 22	17 to 13
15 to 18	17 to 21	9 to 14
24 to 20	22 to 17	22 to 17
11 to 15	15 to 18	1 to 6
28 to 24	26 to 22	32 to 28
8 to 11	18 to 25	5 to 9
26 to 23	29 to 22	27 to 23
9 to 14	11 to 15	15 to 18
31 to 26Var.	13 to 9	19 to 15

18 to 27	23 to 5	32 to 28
15 to 8	15 to 18	10 to 15
14 to 18	26 to 23	27 to 23
8 to 3	18 to 22	22 to 26
W. wins.	25 to 18	18 to 14
	10 to 10	15 to 18
Var.	19 to 10	23 to 19
5 to 9	6 to 22	26 to 31 .
21 to 17	23 to 18	14 to 9
14 to 21	7 to 10	W. wins.

Game XVII.

11 to 15	30 to 26	9 to 14	31 to 26
22 to 17	11 to 15	16 to 11	28 to 24
8 to 11	26 to 17	12 to 16	26 to 22
17 to 13	15 to 18	19 to 12	24 to 27
4 to 8	22 to 14	15 to 18	23 to 18
23 to 19	9 to 38	22 to 15	15 to 19
15 to 18	27 to 23	10 to 28	22 to 17
24 to 20	18 to 27	17 to 10	27 to 23
11 to 15	32 to 23	6 to 15	18 to 14
28 to 24	7 to 11	8 to 11	23 to 18
8 to 11	29 to 25	28 to 32	8 to 4
26 to 23	5 to 9	8 to 4	18 to 9
18 to 22	25 to 22	32 to 28 .	13 to 6
25 to 18	11 to 15	4 to 8	1 to 10
15 to 22	20 to 16	2 to 7	17 to 13

7 to 11	9 to 6	32 to 28	14 to 10
4 to 8	24 to 28	21 to 17	28 to 24
10 to 15	6 to 2	28 to 32	6 to 2
13 to 9	28 to 32	17 to 14	Drawn.
19 to 24	2 to 6	32 to 28	

Game XVIII.

11 to 16	19 to 16	14 to 21	22 to 18
22 to 18	20 to 27	19 to 16	6 to 9
8 to 11	16 to 7	12 to 19	11 to 7
25 to 22	2 to 11	23 to 7	13 to 17
4 to 8	31 to 24	10 to 14	18 to 15
29 to 25	12 to 16	26 to 23	14 to 18
10 to 14	24 to 19	3 to 10	23 to 14
24 to 19	8 to 12	28 to 24	9 to 18
7 to 10	32 to 27	10 to 15	24 to 19
27 to 24	16 to 20	18 to 11	17 to 22
16 to 20	21 to 17	9 to 13	Drawn.

Game XIX.

11 to 16	18 to 15	6 to 10	19 to 15
22 to 18	8 to 12	24 to 19	10 to 19
10 to 14	15 to 11	15 to 24	22 to 17
25 to 22	7 to 10	28 to 19	13 to 22
16 to 20	22 to 18	9 to 13	26 to 10
29 to 25	10 to 15	18 to 9	19 to 26
12 to 16	25 to 22	5 to 14	30 to 23

3 to 8	15 to 19	16 to 19	27 to 31
11 to 7	23 to 18	15 to 10	18 to 14
2 to 11	19 to 23	19 to 24	8 to 11
11 to 7	18 to 15	27 to 23	10 to 7
11 to 15	23 to 26	24 to 27	Drawn.
7 to 3	31 to 22	23 to 18	

CHAPTER VIII.

CRITICAL SITUATIONS AND ENDINGS OF GAMES.

THE endings of games are worthy particular study. Let young players amuse themselves for an hour or two by trying their skill at the following : the men are to be placed in the positions indicated. The White pieces in each case occupy the lower half of the board, and move upward.

WHITE TO MOVE AND DRAW.

Black.	White.
King on 19	King on 32
King on 18	King on 27
Man on 28	

In this position it seems very easy for Black to win ; but White with the move must draw. Try this ; there are not above four moves on each side.

WHITE TO MOVE AND DRAW.

Black.	White.
Man on 5	King on 7
King on 9	

In this situation—one that often occurs in play—it

CRITICAL SITUATIONS.   97

would seem that Black ought to win, from the fact
that he has the advantage of a man, but he cannot
extricate it, and so White is enabled to draw.   Try
this :—

WHITE TO MOVE AND WIN.

Black men on squares 1, 2, 3, 5, 7, 8, 10, 12, 15,
16, and 18.
White men on squares 13, 17, 19, 21, 22, 24, 25,
27, 28, 31, and 32.
This is an instructive position, and will afford the
amateur good practice.
Black men on squares 1, 2, 3, 5, 7, 8, 10, 12, 15,
16, and 18.
White men on squares 13, 17, 19, 21, 22, 24, 25,
27, 28, 31, and 32.

White.	Black.
13 to 9	5 to 14
17 to 13	16 to 23
24 to 19	15 to 24
22 to 6	2 to 9
13 to 6	1 to 10
27 to 9	8 to 11
28 to 19	11 to 16
31 to 27	16 to 23
27 to 18 and wins.	

And again—

13 to 9	16 to 23
17 to 13	5 to 14
24 to 19	15 to 24
22 to 6	1 to 10
27 to 9	8 to 11 and wins.

A few more examples of critical situations will be found useful to the student.

BLACK TO MOVE AND WIN.

White.	Black.
Man on 6	Man on 12
Man on 24	K on 15

WHITE TO MOVE AND WIN.

White.	Black.
K on 14	K on 6
K on 18	K on 14
K on 23	

EITHER SIDE TO MOVE AND WIN.

Black.	White.
K on 26	K on 25
K on 27	Man on 21

Black Kings on squares 19, 18 ; man on square

28. White Kings on 32, 27. White moves and draws, thus—

White.	Black.
27 to 24	18 to 15
24 to 20	15 to 11
20 to 24	19 to 15
24 to 20	

White draws by keeping command of square 20.

PROBLEM I.

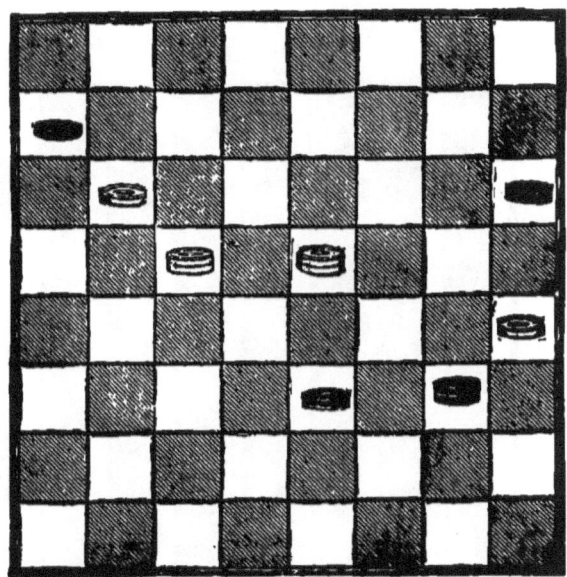

White to move and win.

PROBLEM II.

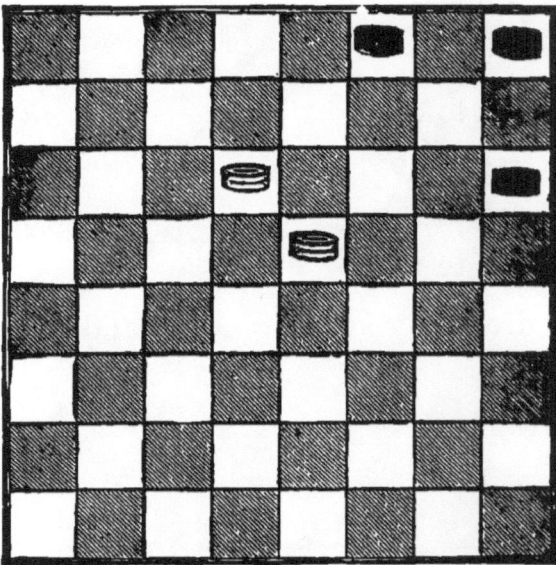

White to move and draw.

PROBLEM III.

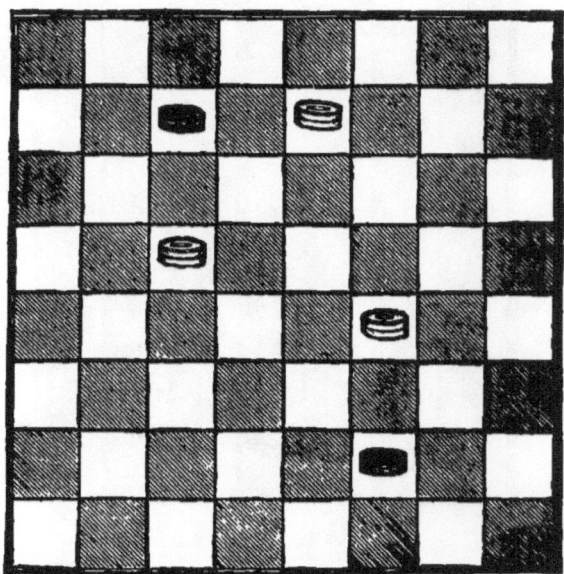

Black to move and White to win.

PROBLEM IV.

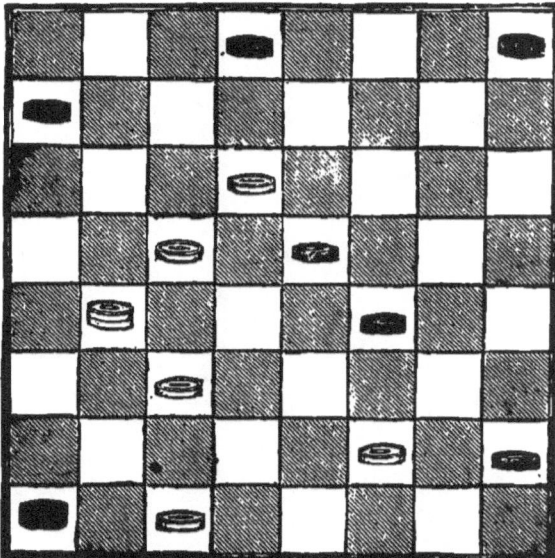

White to move and win.

PROBLEM V.

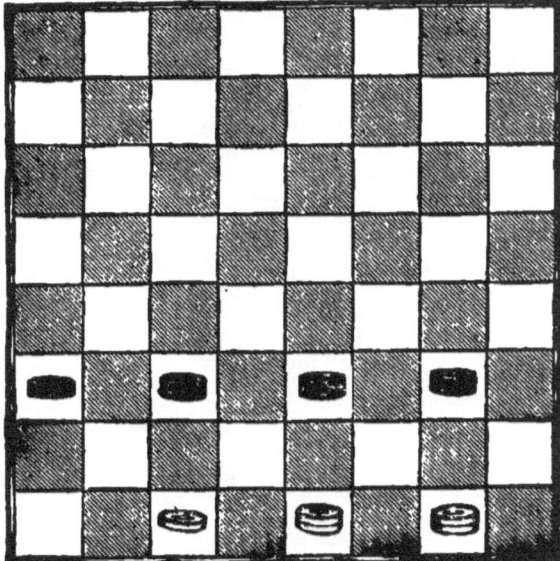

White to move, B. wins ; or Black moves, and White draws.

PROBLEM VI.

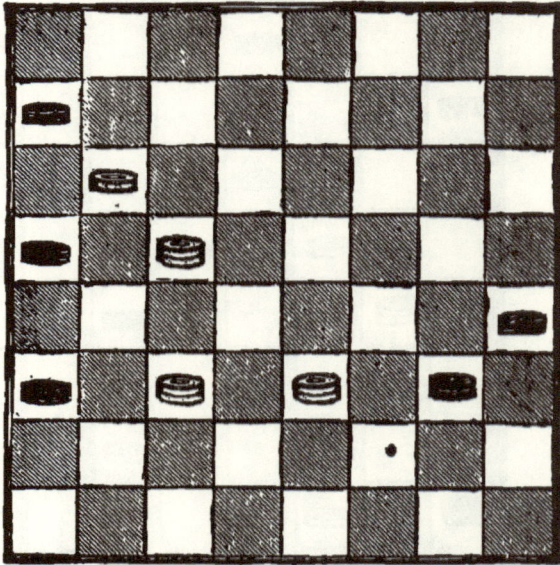

White to move and win.

PROBLEM VII.

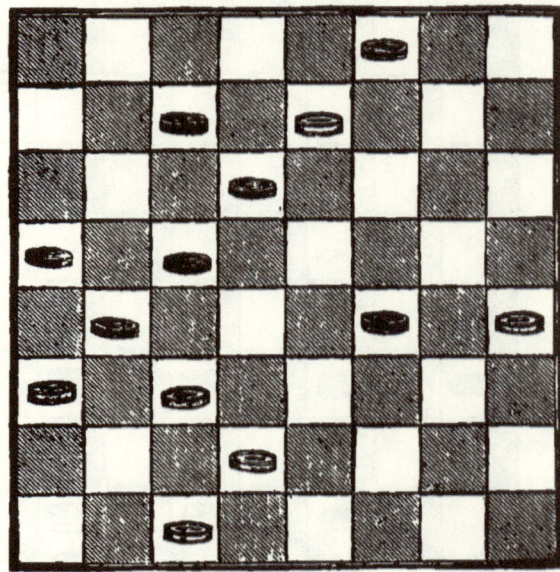

Black to move and win.

PROBLEM VIII.

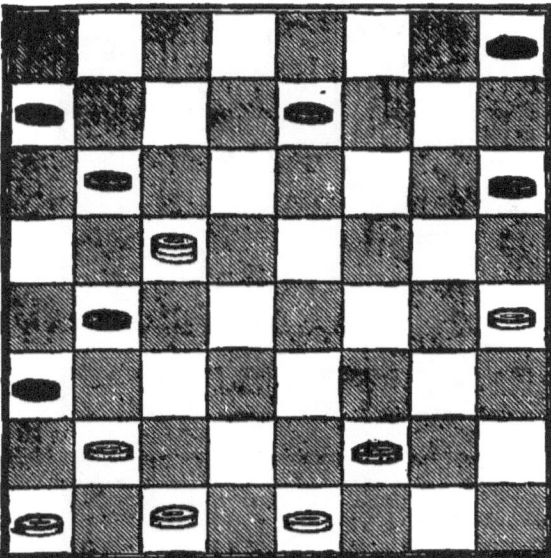

White to move and win.

PROBLEM IX.

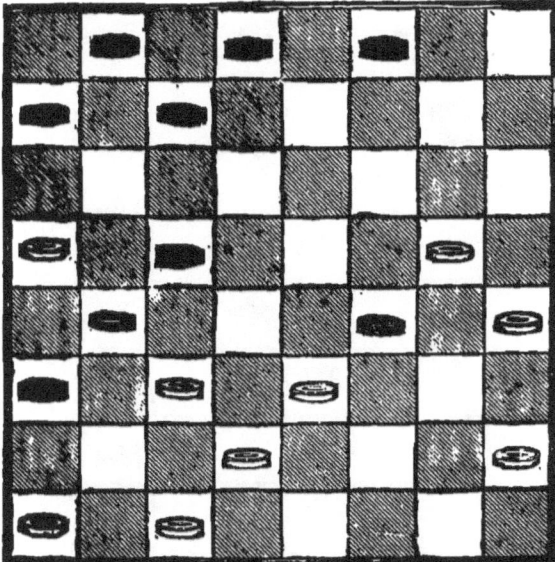

Black to move and win.

DRAUGHTS.

PROBLEM X.

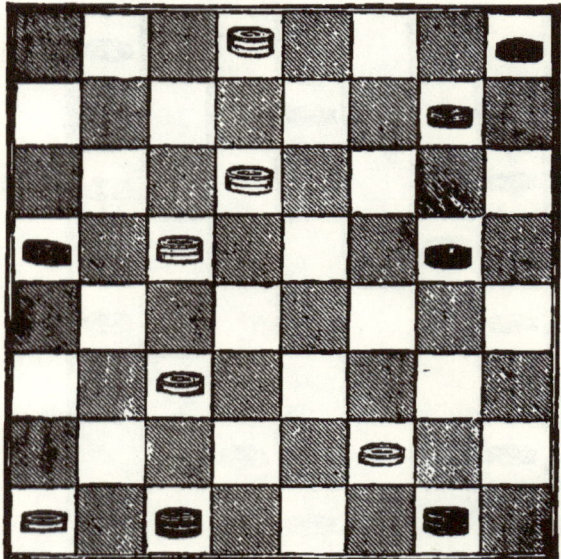

White to move and win.

PROBLEM XI.

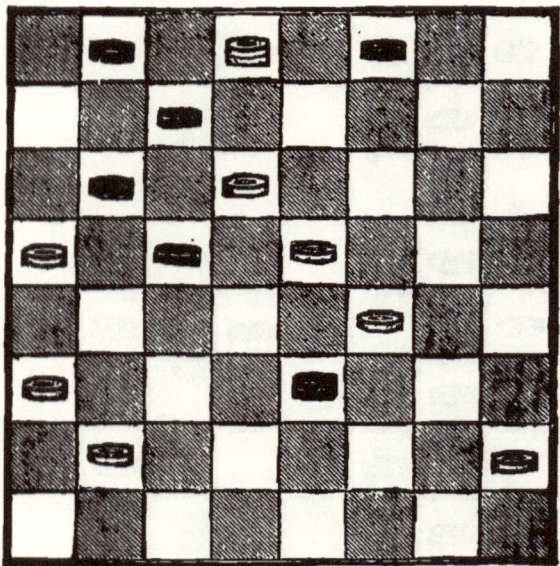

White to move and win.

Problem XII.

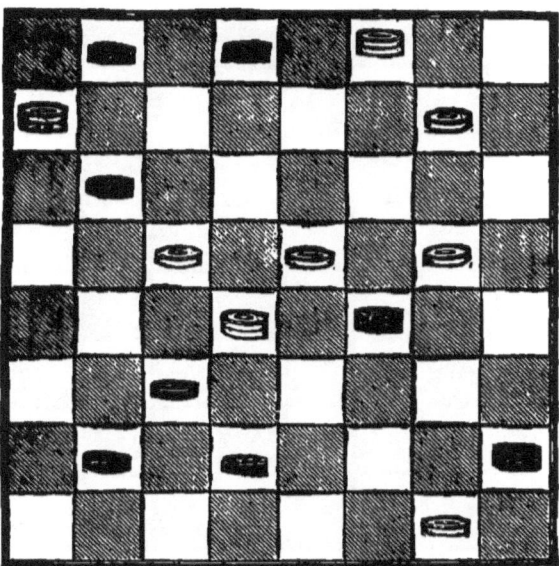

White to move and win.

Problem XIII.

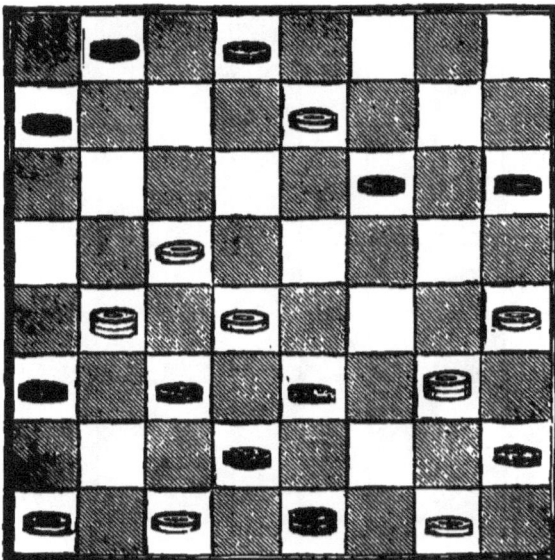

White to move and win.

PROBLEM XIV.

White to move and win.

PROBLEM XV.

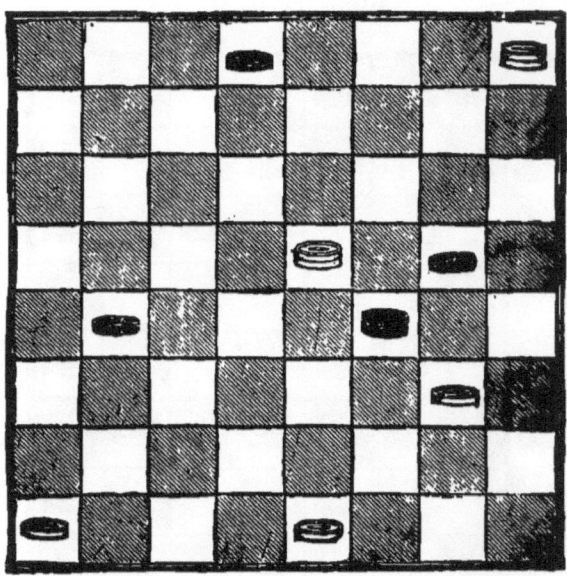

White to move and win.

Problem XVI.

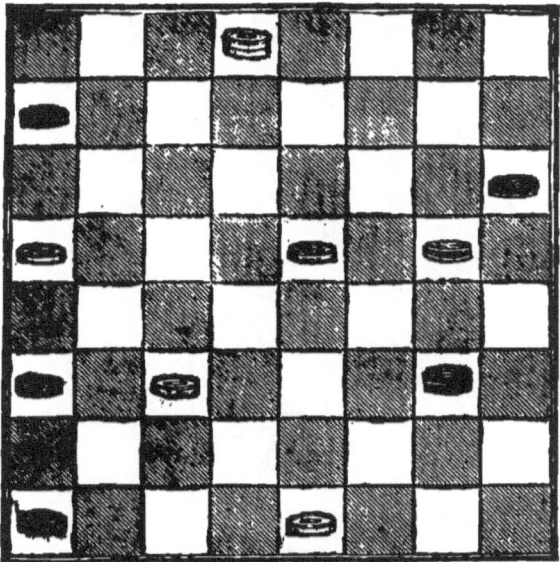

White to move and win.

Problem XVII.

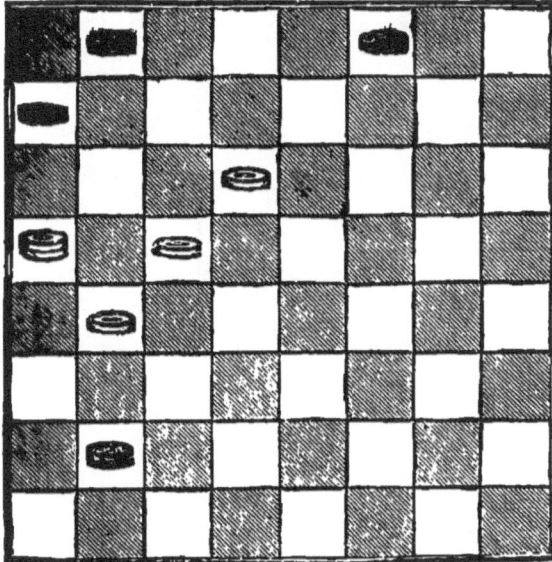

White to move and win.

PROBLEM XVIII.

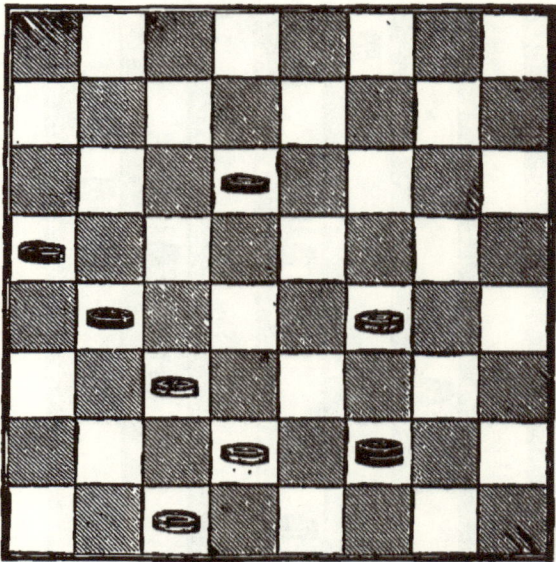

White to move and win.

PROBLEM XIX.

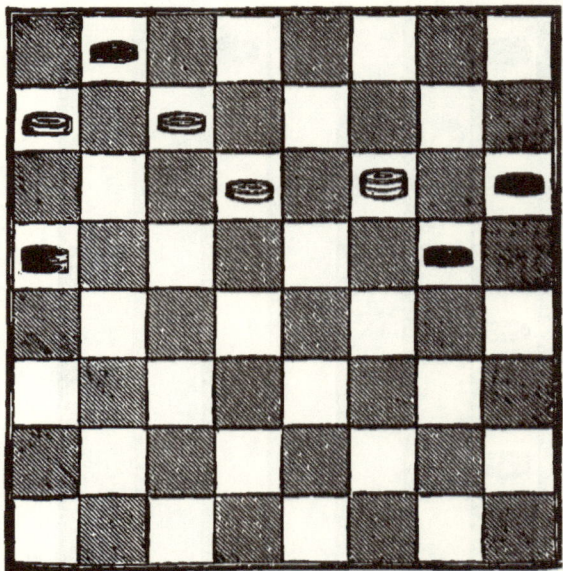

Black to move and win.

PROBLEM XX.

White to move and win.

PROBLEM XXI.

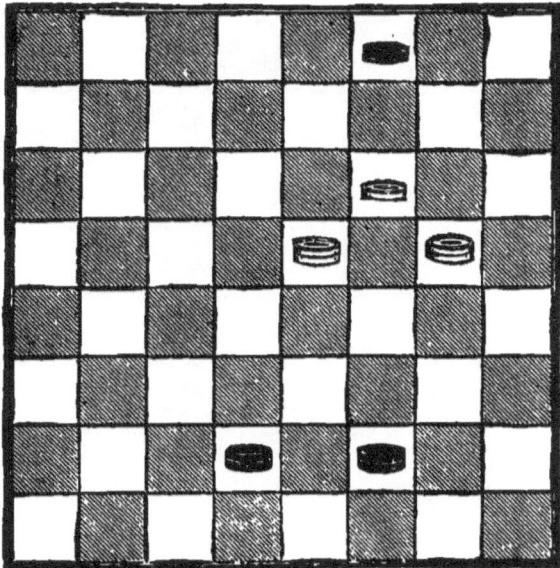

White to move and win.

DRAUGHTS.

PROBLEM XXII.

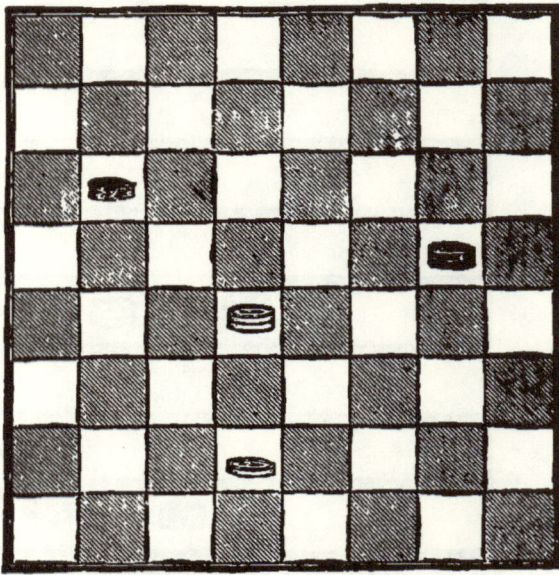

White to move and win.

PROBLEM XXIII.

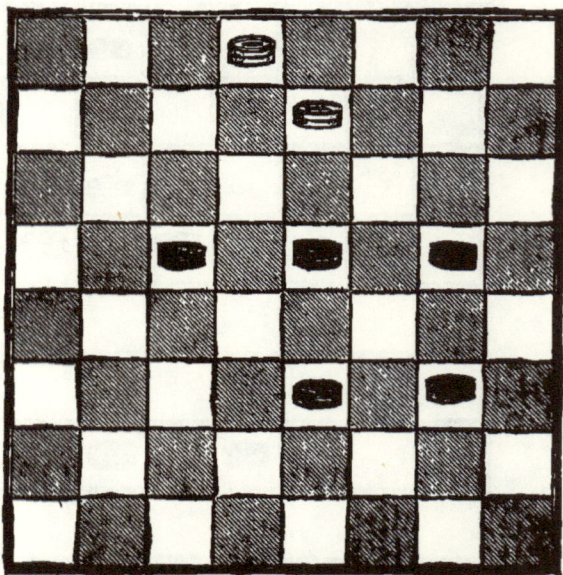

White to move and win.

PROBLEM XXIV.

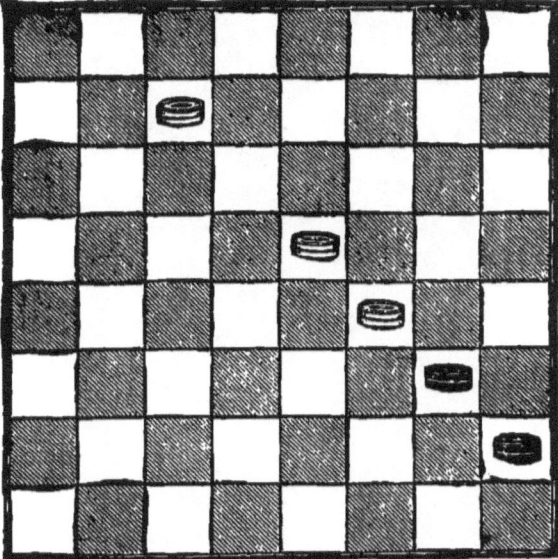

White to move and win.

PROBLEM XXV.

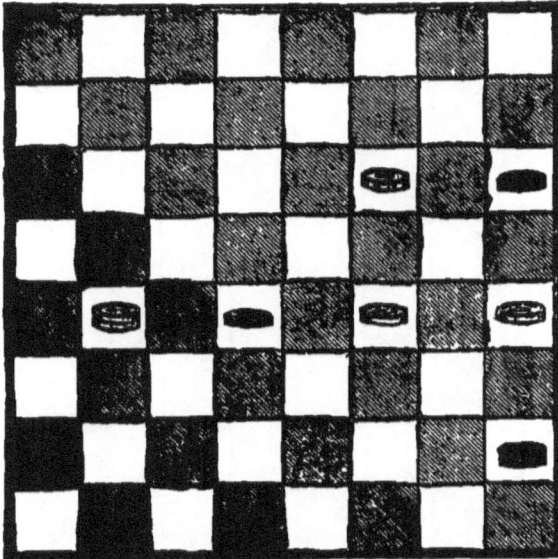

Black to move and White to win.

PROBLEM XXVI.

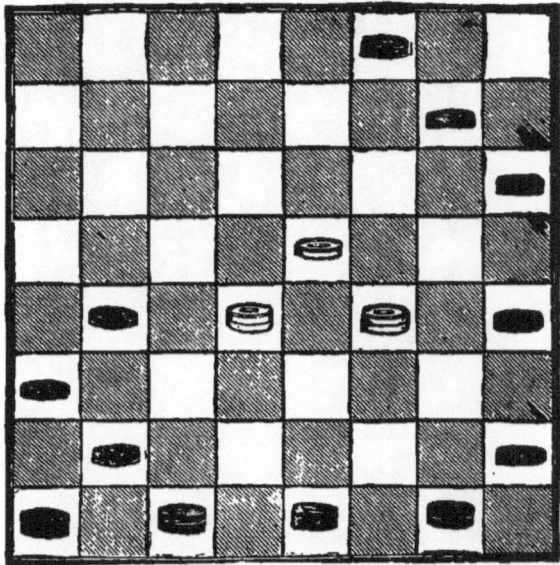

White to move and win.

PROBLEM XXVII.

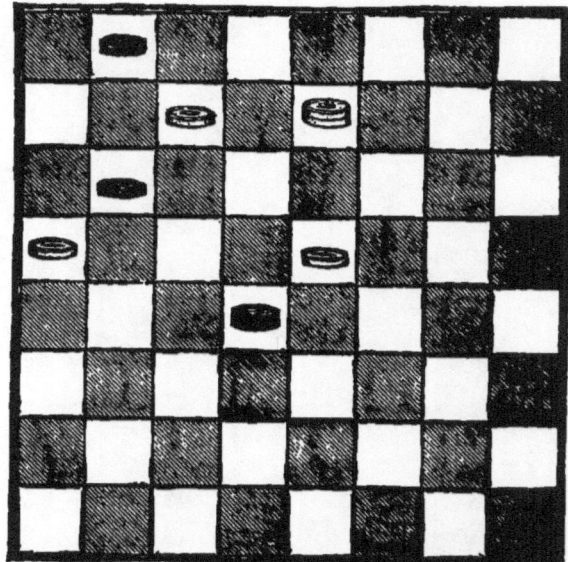

White to move and win.

·Problem XXVIII.

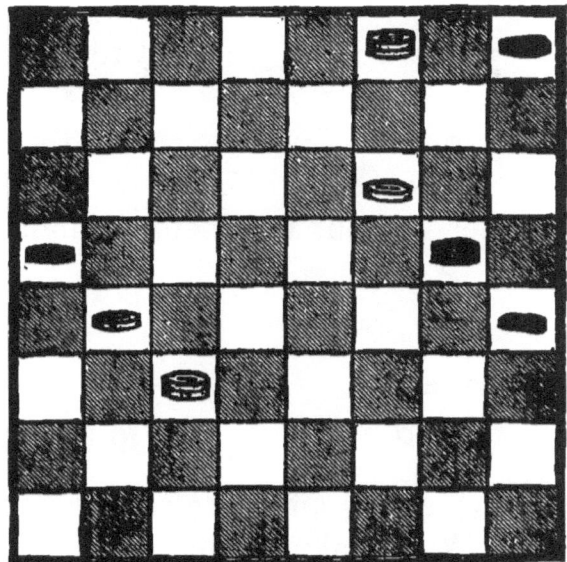

White to move and win.

SOLUTIONS TO PROBLEMS.

Problem I.

The * denotes a piece taken. In each of the Problems the White men move upward.

White.	Black.
20 to 16	12 to 19*
14 to 18	5 to 14*
18 to 20	

Taking man and king. Black loses a man at his next move.

Problem II.

White.	Black.
15 to 11	3 to 8
10 to 15	8 to 3
15 to 19	12 to 8

And so on, Black never being able to get away from the corner without sacrificing a man.

Problem III.

White.	Black.
6 to 10	19 to 23

If Black take the two kings, 27 to 9, he loses immediately, by White taking from 7 to 5. If Black take from 10 to 17, White takes from 23 to 32, and has two kings to one.

Problem IV.

White.	Black.
22 to 18	15 to 22*
17 to 26*	28 to 32 & crowns
27 to 24	19 to 28*
26 to 23	

Black has the advantage of a man, but he must lose, as every piece is blocked, and he loses them successively. This is a very neat solution.

Problem V.

White to move and Black to win.

White.	Black.
32 to 28	24 to 20
28 to 32	22 to 18
31 to 27	23 to 19
27 to 31	19 to 24
32 to 27	24 to 28
27 to 32	18 to 22
31 to 27	22 to 26*
30 to 23	28 to 24

And same position—Black to move and White to draw.

Black.	White.
24 to 28	31 to 27
23 to 19	28 to 31
19 to 24	32 to 27
24 to 20	27 to 32
22 to 18	3 to 27

Problem VI.

23 to 19	24 to 15*
14 to 17	5 to 14
17 to 11	

Taking a man and king, and blocking the rest. Black can sacrifice a man and get a king, but cannot gain the double corner to make a draw.

Problem VII.

19 to 23	26 to 19*
17 to 26*	30 to 23*
14 to 18*	23 to 14
10 to 17	21 to 14
3 to 17	

Leaving Black with three men to two.

Problem VIII.

14 to 10	7 to 14*
20 to 16	12 to 19*
27 to 23	19 to 26*
31 to 6*	

Taking three men and winning.

Problem IX.

Black.	White.
4 to 18	22 to 15*
17 to 22	26 to 17*
19 to 26*	30 to 21*
6 to 9	13 to 6*
1 to 26*	

Taking three men, making a king at his next move, and winning.

Problem X.

29 to 25	32 to 23*
2 to 7	30 to 21*
22 to 17	13 to 22*
14 to 17	12 to 14*
10 to 3*	

Taking five men. A most ingenious series of moves leading up to this result, leaving Black man blocked in 4.

Problem XI.

White.	Black.
25 to 22	23 to 16*
15 to 11	6 to 15*
13 to 6	1 to 10*
28 to 24	16 to 7*
2 to 9	

Taking three and winning.

Problem XII.

15 to 10	19 to 12*
3 to 7	2 to 11*
32 to 27	12 to 3*
27 to 24	28 to 19*
18 to 23	

Now, wherever Black moves, he loses the game.

Problem XIII.

18 to 15	11 to 18*
24 to 19	2 to 11*
20 to 16	11 to 20*
29 to 25	22 to 29*
17 to 22	18 to 25*
19 to 24	20 to 27*
14 to 10	

It will be seen that, by a judicious system of losses, the White is enabled at last to completely block eleven men with a single king. His own men on squares 30 and 32 greatly assist this extraordinary blockade.

Problem XIV.

15 to 11	8 to 15*
30 to 26	22 to 31 king.
32 to 28	31 to 24
28 to 1*	

Takes three men, makes a king, and wins the game in four moves. This is a very neat combination.

Problem XV.

24 to 20	19 to 10*
20 to 11*	10 to 7
29 to 25	7 to 16*
31 to 26	17 to 21
4 to 8	20 to 30* king.
8 to 12	30 to 23*
12 to 26*	

Takes two kings, and wins in three moves.

Problem XVI.

White.	Black.
29 to 25	21 to 30* king.
31 to 26*	30 to 23*
22 to 18	23 to 14*
15 to 10	14 to 7*
2 to 27*	

Wins in four moves.

Problem XVII.

White.	Black.
10 to 6	1 to 10*
14 to 7*	3 to 10*
17 to 14	10 to 17*
13 to 29	

Taking man and king, and winning in three moves.

Problem XVIII.

White.	Black.
26 to 23	17 to 26* (best)
19 to 16	27 to 18*
30 to 7*	

Takes three pieces, and wins.

Problem XIX.

Black.	White.
13 to 9	11 to 20* (best)
9 to 2*	20 to 24
12 to 16	24 to 28
16 to 19	28 to 32
19 to 24	

Problem XX.

White.	Black.
19 to 24	20 to 27*
18 to 22	

A good instance of blockade.

Problem XXI.

White.	Black.
11 to 8	3 to 19*
15 to 22*	

Problem XXII.

White.	Black.
18 to 15	9 to 14
26 to 22	14 to 18
15 to 11	

Problem XXIII.

White moves from 7 to 10, when Black takes the
king and loses. This is introduced merely to show
the position in which two kings may win against
three or more.

Problem XXIV.

White retires to 10, when Black takes and is retaken ; showing how three kings win against two.
The positions in both these problems occur frequently in ordinary play.

Problem XXV.

Black.	White.
28 to 24	20 to 16
24 to 8	17 to 14

Problem XXVI.

White.	Black.
18 to 22	17 to 26
19 to 24	20 to 27

This curious position could not occur in actual
play ; but it is, nevertheless, illustrative.

Problem XXVII.

White moves from 15 to 10, when Black loses in
a few moves.

Problem XXVIII.

White moves from 22 to 18—Black from 13 to 22.

CHAPTER IX.

POLISH DRAUGHTS.

THIS is an interesting variety of the regular game of Draughts. It used to be played on a board of a hundred squares, but the regular English board is now almost universally employed. The men are placed in the same way and the moves are made with the same number of men, precisely as in the English game, but with a difference—the board is placed with a double corner to the right hand of the player, and the men *take either backwards or forwards*. They always move forwards, however, and only take by a backward jump when a man belonging to the adversary is *en prise*. The man must proceed as long as there is a piece that can be taken ; but a man once passed over, cannot be repassed in the course of the same *coup*. It is allowable, however, to pass and repass the same square any number of times, provided the same man is not twice leapt over. In other words, the vacant squares are free to the player, but he cannot twice pass over a covered square. In order that there may be no confusion, in consequence of the intricacy of the moves, the pieces taken are not removed from the board till the move of the attacking man is completed.

Kings are made in the same manner as in the English game, by placing one man on the top of the other. But it must be observed, that the man does not become a King if in the course of his march he arrives at the back square on his opponent's side of the board and there is still another piece that may be taken. In such a case he must continue to take all he can, wherever there is a vacant square between the last man taken and the next man in the same angle.

The player is bound to take all he can legally and practically—there is no huffing ; but if he fails to take the largest number possible, he may be huffed, or compelled to take the men, at the option of his adversary.

The King, in Polish Draughts, is exceedingly powerful. He can traverse the board over all the angles, and take a man lying in the angle. Thus, if he stands on square 1, he may take pieces on squares 19, 26, 21, 7, 16, 27, 17, &c., wherever they are *en prise*, without regard to the number of vacant squares between each man. In fact, his power is precisely that of the Bishop at Chess, with the additional advantage of not pausing when he has taken a man or any number of men.

The advantage of possessing a King is therefore much greater in the Polish than in the English game, as the young player will soon discover. Mr. Bohn, in his essay on Polish Draughts, has the following on the general conduct of the game :

" When a player at the end of the game has a King and a man against three Kings, the best way is to sacrifice the man as soon as possible, because the game is more easily defended with the King alone.

" In Polish Draughts especially, it is by exchanges that good players parry strokes and prepare them ; if the game is embarrassed, they open it by giving man for man, or two for two. If a dangerous stroke is in preparation, they avoid it by exchanging man for man. If it is requisite to strengthen the weak side of your game, it may be managed by exchanging. If you wish to acquire the move, exchange will produce it. Finally, it is by exchanges that one man frequently keeps many confined, and that the game is eventually won.

" When two men of one color are so placed that there is an empty square behind each, and a vacant square between them, where his adversary can place himself, it is called a *lunette,* and this is much more likely to occur in the Polish than in the English game.

" In this position one of the men must necessarily be taken, because they cannot both be played, nor escape at the same time. The lunette frequently offers several men to be taken on both sides. As it is most frequently a snare laid by a skilful player, it must be regarded with suspicion ; for it is not to be supposed that the adversary, if he be a practised player, would expose himself to lose one or more men for nothing. Therefore, before entering the lunette, look at your adversary's position, and then calculate what you yourself would do in a similar position. Towards the end of a game, when there are but few pawns left on the board, concentrate them as soon as possible.

"At that period of the game the slightest error is fatal. The King is so powerful a piece, that one, two, or three pawns may be advantageously sacrificed to obtain him. But in doing so, it is necessary to note the future prospects of his reign. Be certain that he will be in safety, and occupy a position that may enable him to retake an equivalent for the pawns sacrificed without danger to himself. An expert player will endeavor to snare the King as soon as he is made, by placing a pawn in his way, so as to cause his being retaken."

———

These are the only games of Draughts played in Europe, but I believe there are several modifications in the game as played by the natives of various parts of India and China. Bayard Taylor, the American traveller, gives an account of Chess and Draughts in Japan ; and, curiously enough, we find that the latter game was played by the aborigines of New Zealand in precisely the Japanese manner. A vast deal of learned research has been expended as to the origin of these games of skill and calculation. Chess has gradually improved into its present scientific aspect ; but Draughts, being simpler in its method, and capable of less variety and modification, has probably remained in much the same condition for centuries. Nevertheless, as a mental exercise and a relaxation from physical toil, Draughts is a capital game. Its main principles may be learned in an hour, while its practice provides reasonable amusement for a lifetime.

www.ingramcontent.com/pod-product-compliance
Lightning Source LLC
Chambersburg PA
CBHW032012010726
47493CB00007B/2369